THE SPIDER:
THE FLAME MASTER

MASTER OF MEN!

THE FLAME MASTER

By Grant Stockbridge

ALTUS PRESS • 2019

PUBLISHING HISTORY

"The Flame Master" originally appeared in the October, 1935 (Vol. 5, No. 2) issue of
The Spider magazine. Copyright 2019 by Argosy Communications, Inc. All rights
reserved.

CHAPTER 1
MAN-MADE LIGHTNING

WITH A single, swift gesture, Richard Wentworth cut the lights and ignition of his car. His foot stabbed the brake. The auto jerked to an abrupt halt as he stared, first with eyes wide, then narrowed keenly, at the hood. Will-o'-the-wisp flames danced over it—little blue points of fire that flickered, leaped high into the air and vanished—to reappear a half second later at another point. In the sudden quiet after the motor was stilled and the tires silent, they made a small fierce crackling.

With a sharp curse rasping in his throat, Wentworth grabbed for the door-latch. His hand flinched away from it and through him tingled the chill of an electric shock! The Devil! There was no time to lose. He had come searching criminals who were playing with man-made lightning and here… He doubled his legs under him, seized a cloth strap across the ceiling and vaulted clear.

Instantly, then, he flung himself flat, wriggling into the underbrush that crowded close.

A gust of wind rustled the leaves, sent small eddies of dust whispering across the unpaved road. Distantly there came the mutter of thunder. That was the only sound save the rasping double croak of a tree-frog far off in the summer woods—and the thin, brittle crackling of the electric fire. The fresh, exhilarating tang of ozone was in the air.

Softly, Wentworth eased to his feet and made his crouching, soundless way into the cover of the woods which was just awakening with the murmur of the storm-wind. Suddenly he flung flat to the earth. Blue-white fire illuminated the woods with flashlight lividness. A crashing explosion beat upon his ears,

hammered on his senses. Half-blinded, wholly deaf, he rolled over and stared back toward the road.

The flames playing over his car were no longer blue. They were orange and golden and they licked higher and higher in flapping tongues. The roadster had been smashed into debris by a lightning bolt!

Yet the mutter of the approaching storm was still far distant. The stir of the storm-wind was just beginning. Wentworth's lips shrank back from his teeth in a thin smile.

Man-made lightning! He had come to the right place!

Swiftly, quietly as a shadow, he thrust his way more deeply into the woods. Unless he was entirely wrong in his guess—and the electric blast confirmed it—men would dash to the wreckage. They would be men hungry for his life, the life of the Spider!

For Richard Wentworth was a nemesis of the night, a swift and secret avenger who meted out lethal justice to those of the underworld who dared to raise their hand against humanity; he was the man known throughout half the civilized world as the Spider. And tonight he wore the disguise that would instantly identify him as that dread killer. A long, black cape covered twisted shoulders. A broad-brimmed hat tightly pulled down over a lank wig shadowed a beak-nosed face. The eyes that glittered there were steely with bitter hatred.

The Spider was hunting tonight a wanton murderer, a slaughterer who had enslaved the very lightnings!

Frozen against the black bole of a tree, he waited for a full two minutes; but no one, nothing save the rustling wind, stirred in the woods.

Presently he pushed on again, dropping silently down a steep slope to a rill that tinkled icily; he went slowly up another more gentle grade. Abruptly, he paused again, pressing close against a tree. The woods ahead were black, as black as the death that might await him there. But at one point, fitful yellow rays of light from a lonely, cottage window made a spot of lesser darkness. Against that moved the figure of a man. It paced slowly, silently forward as if to meet the Spider!

Wentworth drew in the skirt of his long black cape so the wind no longer rustled it dully against his legs. He breathed lightly through his mouth. Behind him, the tree-frog made an experimental croak, hesitated and took up its monotonous song. Wentworth—the Spider—waited.

THAT ISOLATED cottage, whose light he saw dimly was the one he must enter to test the full accuracy of his suspicions. The man who lived there was Brandon Early, whom newspapers had christened: "The Earl of the Electrons." It was natural that the Spider's keen mind should turn to this young genius of electrical experimentation when a bolt of lightning assisted criminals to escape. That lightning had blasted six policemen into instant, charred death and permitted a gang of bank robbers to get away with nearly one-hundred-thousand dollars.

It was not that Early had an evil reputation, but he had been experimenting diligently with lightning for months. Everyone in the scientific world knew that. If he had no hand in the crimes, at least he should be able to indicate who might have stolen his secrets. So Wentworth thought. Now, awaiting that dimly seen figure, automatic gripped solidly in his hand,

Wentworth decided there was little doubt that Early was deeply involved. That blast of lightning, smashing his car cunningly, was no accident!

The figure—it was a cautiously moving man the Spider saw—continued its slow advance. Two yards away it halted.

"*Sahib?*" the word was hardly more than a mere sigh of the wind.

The Spider stepped out into the man's path. Instantly the fellow bowed, his movement a dim shifting of shadows. Wentworth smiled faintly. He knew that Ram Singh, his faithful Hindu servant, was rising cupped hands to his turbaned forehead in a salaam, though he sensed rather than saw the movement. Even in this darkness, in the shadow of death itself, the Hindu would not forsake the formalities, the respect, due his master.

His salaam completed, Ram Singh stepped closer, his usually strong, nasal voice cut to a whisper: "*Sahib,*" he murmured, "the wood is full of men. I counted eleven and heard sounds indicating almost as many more."

Wentworth's smile hardened, his lips pressing cold against his teeth. Were they police or criminals, these twenty-two men about Brandon Early's home? It did not matter. Police and criminals would be equally anxious for the Spider's death.

For an entire month now, ever since his gallant servitor and friend, Jackson, had laid down his life for Wentworth, the Spider had made no appearance. Jackson had worn the Spider disguise at his death, had confessed all the Spider's crimes and thus lifted deadly suspicion from Wentworth's head. But the underworld, freed of its terrible fear of that swift avenger of the night, had begun to strike wantonly again at humanity.

It was necessary that the Spider be resurrected. The underworld must feel once more the steel of his wrath, must know anew that he stood as a shield between them and the humanity to whose protection he had pledged his life.

Yes, criminals had ample reason for their bitter hate, and the police in addition considered him not a defender of the innocent, but a merciless killer. The law could not overlook the fact that he killed only those who richly merited his swift justice. It was murder, identical with any other homicide, to them. And their search was spurred on by a growing hatred for the mysterious avenger of the night who eluded their most elaborate traps with mocking ease; who solved and punished crimes with a speed that made their own efforts ridiculous by contrast.

No, it did not matter whether this ambuscade comprised criminals or police. Their guns were equally hungry for the Spider's blood. Wentworth touched Ram Singh lightly, reassuringly on the arm.

"I am going to enter that house, Ram Singh," he said softly. "Do nothing unless I call for you, but in the meantime creep as close as possible without disturbing the watchman."

"But, *sahib!*" Ram Singh's voice was disturbed. "Twenty-two men! They have formed a double cordon about the cottage. It is impossible to get through without being discovered."

Wentworth laughed softly. When he spoke again it was in staccato Hindustani. "To that man who has courage in his heart, only failure is impossible," he quoted an ancient Sikh proverb. "It is a command!" he finished sharply.

Once more he caught dim movement and knew that Ram Singh had salaamed. "I hear and obey, *sahib.*"

WENTWORTH SLIPPED on toward the light that marked the house. His movements were infinitely cautious now. Each time he set down his foot, his toe first carefully brushed the spot clean of twigs or rocks that might make a sound to cause an alarm. When he passed through shrubbery, the switches that might rustle against him were bent aside carefully, then allowed to straighten silently behind him. Twenty-two men, any of whom would gladly welcome the chance to kill him!

The Spider nodded slightly as he gently removed a rotten branch from beneath his right foot and wriggled it, toe first, into the leaves. This strong guard was a further confirmation of his suspicions! Man-made lightning! It seemed ridiculous on the face of it. But it had seemed absurd also to think that lightnings from the sky had intervened in the chase of those bandits, had smashed his car to bits.

Police had surrounded the brick bank of Derbytown after a passerby had spotted the criminals at work inside. Just as the marauders rushed from the place, a bolt of lightning had smashed into a car in which police waited... and the bandits had made good their escape.

Brandon Early's cottage was within fifty yards of Wentworth now, a ghostly, white glimmer against the night. There was a large combination garage and workshop off to the right and Wentworth could discern a single watchman stationed beside it. No others were in sight, yet with twenty-two men in two cordons, assuming even distribution, there must be at least five men to each of the four sides of the house.

That meant Wentworth would probably have to overcome at least four men to reach the cottage, and even then his capture—or at least the discovery that some one had pierced the lines—would be only a matter of moments! It was a perilous spot, but the Spider did not for a moment consider retreat. It would be possible to return another time and see Brandon Early, of course, but this extra-heavy guard indicated to Wentworth's agile mind that some new deviltry was afoot within. He was determined to learn its nature.

Slowly, he circled to his left, keeping well within the fringe of the woods, searching for a guard. He located one presently, leaning against a tree. At first no more than part of the freakish trunk, silhouetted obscurely against the white sides of the house, he betrayed his reality presently by a slight, hacking cough.

Wentworth swiftly drew a length of silken rope from a pocket in his cape. It was light, scarcely the diameter of a pencil, but it would stand a strain of seven-hundred pounds. The Spider's nimble fingers made a slip-noose while his eyes searched out a lone bare branch overhead.

He knew that he could not lasso the guard while he leaned against the tree. Neither could he creep forward until he could overpower the man so silently that he would not be detected by watchful ears. But he had a plan, and he proceeded with it as calmly as if the twenty-two men who would kill him on sight were nowhere about him.

When his noose was ready, he flung it over the tree-limb and held both loop and whip-end in his hands. He curled surplus rope with the loop, then, behind another tree, he laughed softly aloud.

It was not the normal, amused laughter of a man. There was a flat, muted quality in it—a sinister mockery that made it eerie— as though it sang weirdly through the midnight from some other fearful world.

The guard stiffened away from the tree with a muffled curse, whirling toward Wentworth. Before he could snap on the flashlight he gripped in his hand, the Spider cast his noose. It settled neatly over the man's head and Wentworth threw his full weight onto the loose end of the rope.

The guard was hauled clear of the ground instantly. He swept through the air in a long arc, whose pivot was the limb above Wentworth's head. The Spider had planned well. The guard's feet could not thrash in the brush, as they would have had he not been lifted clear of earth. His voice was choked in his throat. The only sound was a faint creaking of the limb above, swallowed in the moan of the wind, and the sodden thump of the flashlight falling to earth. Neither raised an alarm.

WENTWORTH CLUNG to the rope until the struggles of the man in the noose weakened. Then he lowered him swiftly to the earth and loosened the cord. Regardless of his reputation, the Spider was no wanton killer. He slew only in self-defense or when, after due deliberation, he decided that a man's crimes warranted death. He had no quarrel with this guard. So he eased the noose and swiftly bound the guard's hands and feet.

From the man's pocket, he swiftly removed a revolver. He wedged it into the crotch of a tree in such a way that a backward pull would only drag it more securely into place. Then he fastened a cord to the gun's trigger, drew it taut, and knotted the other end to his prisoner's hand-bonds.

For another brief moment, the Spider squatted beside his prey. He pressed the base of a gleaming cigarette lighter to the man's forehead, then straightened and loped away. The man was already beginning to stir. When he awakened, he would find upon his forehead a splotch like a curse in blood, a thing with sprawling hairy legs and poised fangs, *the seal of the Spider!*

Wentworth had rarely fixed his seal upon a living man, but he wished to spread again the terror of the Spider; to shout aloud once more that the underworld needs must seek cover from his all-seeing vengeance. A live man, branded with his ineradicable seal, would help accomplish that.

When Wentworth was in the shadows of the underbrush, nearest the out-building, he paused again and crouched to hide. The guard he had spotted there still stood against the wall. The Spider's trap was prepared. He would have to wait only until the guard he had strangled should regain partial consciousness.

He did not have long to wait. Before a minute passed, the bound man had yanked on his bonds and discharged the revolver in the tree crotch. Instantly, the guard against the wall snatched out a gun and darted toward the sound. Two more shots crashed out. Wentworth laughed soundlessly, and stole swiftly to the cottage, found a basement window. A kick broke the latch. All about him was alarm and wild turmoil. The sound he made would scarcely be noticed.

Quickly lowering himself into the cellar, Wentworth fixed the window-catch so that it would not show the break, then concealed himself rapidly among a forest of furnace pipes. For half an hour, he waited during a noisy cursing search of the woods. It terminated only when the storm broke with a rushing beat of wind-driven rain. Finally all was quiet again and the Spider emerged from his hiding place and located the stairs.

At the door at the head of the steps he crouched and listened for a long minute. He could hear a muffled grumble of voices, but he saw the room just beyond the door was dark. He eased up the latch noiselessly and peered through the crack. To his right, a thread of light showed under another door. The gruff voices came from there. Soundlessly, Wentworth stole toward it.

Suddenly, without warning, the room blazed with brilliant light. Wentworth whirled, dodged aside and snapped out his gun. But he did not fire. Instead, he stood with eyes widening in astonishment.

A man crouched across the room. He had the body of a powerfully built man, but the face was scarcely human in any aspect. The eyes glittered like those of an animal, a tuft of reddish whiskers bearded the chin and the forehead was creased in a leonine frown. Even more amazing, a great reddish-black mane brushed upward and backward from the nape of his neck. For an instant, Wentworth was paralyzed by the thought that this creature charging across the room had the body of a man and the head of a lion!

Even as he thrust that idea from his brain as ridiculous, the creature sprang toward him. In one prodigious bound, he was in the air, his hands drawn back to strike, not as a man would hit with his fists, but as a lion would rake with talons! *And there were claws on that man's hands!*

Frantically, Wentworth jerked up his automatic, squeezing on the trigger. He did not hear the gun explode. A blow caught him from behind, smashing him to the floor, crashing out his sense in a million scintillant points of dancing light.

CHAPTER 2
THE LION MAN

BEING UNCONSCIOUS was no new experience to Wentworth. A man does not spend his entire life fighting vicious criminals and never meet with a knockout tap on the head. The Spider had learned control of his reflexes. Consequently, when he became gradually aware again of his environment, he repeated his usual trick of feigning continued unconsciousness. But this time it didn't fool anyone.

"All right, Spider!" a deep voice growled. "That stimulant has had plenty of chance to take effect. Open your eyes!"

Wentworth heard the words through the pound and ache of his brain, but he forced a small smile to his lips and obeyed. His mind was racing now with the memory of what he had last seen—a man with a leonine head and *claws on his hands!* That last seemed fantastic, utterly absurd, but Wentworth had fought too long against criminal madmen to consider anything impossible. He was wondering as he opened his eyes whether....

The first thing he saw was the Lion Man. There was nothing else to call him. Wentworth stared at him with an outward appearance of calm that was far from revealing his true feelings. Out of the corners of his eyes, he had seen that four other men were in the room, men who leveled automatics and whose eyes glittered with hatred: the hatred of the underworld for the Spider! A tension quivered in his muscles, an involuntary bracing for the shock of expected bullets. He fought down the pounding of his heart and studied the Lion Man.

He appeared truly formidable—six feet one of whipcord manhood. Closer scrutiny increased the first, quick impression that he was a hybrid of beast and human. He was smiling with a slight, stiff uplift of his mouth-corners. Wentworth thought he had never seen a more cruel countenance nor one that showed a greater potentiality for evil.

The smile did not lighten the leonine vertical creases between his eyes. The mane was incredibly profuse, hanging down almost to his shoulders. Strands of it, thick and coarse, drooped in front of his ears. The Spider saw, with a start of surprise that he barely suppressed, that the reddish mustaches were stippled by a half-dozen long, stiff spikes of hair, jutting out horizontally like a cat's whiskers!

Irresistibly, Wentworth lifted his head from the floor to see the hands. They hung idly at the Lion Man's sides, fingers curved inward, palms toward the back. If there were claws upon them, they were effectually concealed. It was all credible enough—all these details could be faked, including the claws. But what in heaven's name was the purpose of such a masquerade? Those cat's whiskers, thrusting out stiffly through his beard. It was ridiculous, but Wentworth felt no urge to laugh. Those intent, bestial eyes looked hungry! Nevertheless, Wentworth dropped his head back on the floor and laughed.

"Where's the masquerade party?" he jeered.

"The knowledge would do you no good, Spider," the Lion Man said smoothly. "You won't be able to go, wherever it is." He paused, lost momentarily in thought. "This certainly is a surprise. We thought the Spider was dead, after Jackson confessed to all the crimes when he died a month or so ago. That grandstand finish of his seemed to clear you satisfactorily, although it is true that there were rumors—that a few of us still suspected you." He stopped again, and then said: "This is capital luck! We have the Spider, and you were the Spider all along, eh, Wentworth?"

WENTWORTH CONTINUED his laughter. "Of course," he agreed. He knew his admission would puzzle them much more than a denial. They would figure that if he were Wentworth, he would not be likely to admit being the Spider. The tightening of the Lion Man's animal eyes confirmed his psychology. "It makes no difference," the maned man said abruptly. "It is still good luck for us. It's too bad for you that the Spider ever came back to life. I dare say you won't be able to do it again, with bullet holes through your heart and brain."

The Spider rolled his head to take in the four gangsters ranged about him with their ready guns, and he laughed once

more as if in quiet amusement. It
was sheer bravado, that laughter;
it was clear courage. He would
laugh still while deadly bullets
thudded into his body. But that
did not mean he failed to recognize the seriousness of his situation. He was in deadly peril. The
palms of his hands were moist.
This man might disguise himself
in foolish fashion, but his weap-

ons would be as sure and as deadly as any other man's.

Actually, the Lion Man needed no weapons. All he had to
do was leave the room, or lift his restraining hand from these
four gunmen and the Spider would die in seconds. Wentworth
noticed that one man bore the red, sprawling Spider seal upon
his forehead and that his throat was bandaged where the silken
noose had burned the flesh.

Wentworth nodded toward him casually, while the throbbing
of his heart became high and strangling: "Glad to make your
acquaintance more formally!"

The guard snarled; his gun hand quivered.

"No!" the Lion Man snarled. He did not look toward the
guard, but the man's cowering side glance told of abject fear
and stern discipline.

"Your guards aren't very clever, Leo," Wentworth addressed
the Lion Man. "I had no trouble at all in penetrating their lines."
He began to describe how he had slipped past the cordons. The

Lion Man's eyes never left his face. Wentworth was thinking furiously as he spoke. He knew that his purpose of gaining time was entirely obvious to the maned man, but as long as he was permitted to continue, that did not matter. A try at his hands told that they were tightly bound. His feet were untied, but lying on the floor, he could not take advantage of that.

His gaze roamed over the room as he talked. He was in the kitchen. The door to the basement was just behind Lion-face. If he could signal Ram Singh... He shouted out swift words in Hindustani and no one attempted to stop him.

"Your Hindu servant is a prisoner in the other room," the Lion Man purred.

Each word thudded into Wentworth's brain like a bullet. Ram Singh was out of the fight! Then, indeed, the Spider was doomed. With the recognition of his helplessness, a terrible calm descended upon Wentworth. Was this, then, the end of all his gallant fights—that he be murdered while he lay flat on his back? Dim thoughts flitted through his brain. A woman's name. Nita! Nita van Sloan to whom his love was pledged. Ram Singh, helpless prisoner, too. He also would be killed.

Wentworth realized that if he were slain here, there would be no one to reveal the fact, now self-evident, that criminals had wrested the secret of man-made lightning from Brandon Early and were prepared to use the weapon against humanity.

Wentworth studied the Lion Man's face and found it as completely merciless and lacking in humane feeling as if indeed he were the hybrid he seemed, with the soul of a great, cruel cat in his part-human body. A chill raced through Wentworth's body that brought shivering tension to all his muscles. He read the Lion Man's swift determination to kill him at once. It showed in the cold flame of the man's eyes. He saw the clawed hand half-lift to signal his end.

"Chief!" a gunman croaked hoarsely. "Chief, leave me be the one to finish him, will ya, chief?"

THE VOICE seemed foolishly like a child's begging for an ice-cream cone—the boon of being allowed to murder! Wentworth knew without turning his head that the man speaking was the one who would forever wear a Spider seal upon his forehead. He thought desperately. If he could only delay the fatal blow for moments… Every heart-beat of time increased the opportunity for something new to develop. Wentworth could see no possibility of escape, but he had won out of equally tight spots before, simply by refusing to abandon hope, by seizing every slight opportunity.

"Please, leave me rub him out, Chief," the gunman whined again. "He put that damned seal on my forehead and it won't never come off…."

"Sure, Leo," Wentworth chuckled, "let a coward kill the Spider. Let the man who couldn't stand up to the Spider in the open kill him now that he's helpless, flat on his back."

The Lion Man's eyes were rigidly fixed on Wentworth, anger blazing in them. There was a stiff tension in the right arm….

"Go ahead, Leo," Wentworth urged, "a craven cur surely is the one who deserves the honor of killing the Spider."

"Please, Chief," the gunman whined again. There was a

persistent eagerness in his voice. He trembled with his desire to kill. It made his voice a hoarse whisper. "Leave me kill him...."

The Lion Man lifted his great head with its mane of hair and looked at the man. Wentworth tensed on the floor. His feet were free. If he could foment a squabble... Without even the warning of bent knees, the Lion Man leaped. His stiffened right arm swept in a wide, swinging arc and slapped against the head and jaw of the branded gunman. Even as the blow landed—as the man's whining words broke off in a wild scream—Wentworth rolled to his knees, then to his feet. Behind him, the scream broke off in a horrid, strangling gurgle.

Wentworth whirled. The gunmen and the Lion Man were between him and the room's three doors, but just to the left of that group was the blank glass of a window. The three gunmen were staring, white-faced, at their companion. He reeled on his feet, hands clutching the left side of his face as though he held in place something that had torn loose. Blood pumped out between his fingers, squeezed between his palms.

The man pitched to the floor, writhing.

"I do not like failures," the Lion Man murmured softly.

As he spoke, Wentworth made his swift decision. That rain-washed window was about seven feet above the ground. Diving through the glass would slash him horribly, but it was a chance against death, a chance to escape and gain freedom to fight this monster. If he plunged through the window head-first, somersaulting as he went, he might be able to land on his shoulders and avoid injury. Swift as was his decision, Wentworth's action was even swifter.

It flashed through his mind that even if he failed in the leap, he might infuriate the Lion Man so that the creature would not decree an instantaneous death. He might prefer to torture the Spider. And torture took time. It might develop opportunities.

He took two strides and still the men had not marked his movement. One more pace and he could dive for the window. He lifted his foot for that third step, doubling forward for the leap. He heard a startled outcry from the men, then, but they were still dazed with horror. They could not even jerk up their guns in time to fire.

Wentworth's right foot hit the floor for the third stride. He sucked in his breath, dived straight into the pane of glass—and was checked in mid-spring! A savage blow caught him on the left shoulder. Needles of pain-fire stabbed through it. Then he crashed to the floor, felt a man's knees gouge sharply into his back.

The knees were jerked away. His body was hauled half-erect, and a wet ripping sound was close to his ear. A shudder wrenched over him as he crouched, half on his knees, hands lashed behind him. He knew now what had struck him—knew why he could not fall to the floor. The Lion Man's claws were embedded deep in his shoulder!

THE REALIZATION of what had happened burned into Wentworth's brain. He knew that within instants, when those fiendish claws were withdrawn and the air got into his wound, tormenting pain would assail him. After that would come nausea and weakness. But for this moment, he was still master of his faculties. He could still fight, perhaps gain more precious seconds of life. With a surge he regained his feet despite the wrenching tear of the claws. He jerked up his right knee savagely into the Lion Man's groin.

The claw ripped free and pain washed over the Spider, twisted like a knife in his heart. Once more he hurled himself toward the window, but two of the gunmen were there before him. He battered into a solid wall of flesh and reeled back. Agony overwhelmed him. He sagged to the floor.

The Lion-faced one's voice came to him as from a great distance: "No, don't kill him with your guns! Tie his feet, and let him wait and suffer. Shooting would be too merciful and quick...."

Wentworth scarcely felt the ropes bite into his ankles, nor the kicks and blows the gunmen rained upon him. He was in a daze of pain, but his mind clamored for escape. He felt himself dragged across the floor; his feet were lashed to the drainpipe of the sink. Then heavy shoes tramped from the room, but one pair of feet still moved lightly in the room, like the lithe tread-ing of a cat.

Slowly the acute agony of Wentworth's wound subsided and for a while he was shaken by resultant nausea. Presently that went too, and he lay still, panting and weak from the loss of seeping blood. He had gained time, but at what a cost! His strength was oozing from him every second. He stared about him frantically. Except for the corpse across the room, he was alone. From the other room came the rumble of voices. Once he heard a shout, a woman's shrill, angry voice.

"You're a murdering thief! I won't do it!" she declared emphatically.

Wentworth frowned—and shook his head dazedly. Someone else was caught in the Lion Man's power.

The blood was still trickling, warm and awful, from Wentworth's torn shoulder. He realized that this was the fleeting chance to escape for which he had fought. Soon, the Lion Man would come back to begin his torture and death. This was the sole opportunity to save himself—to save humanity from this fearful scourge of man-made lightning. His one chance! Weak, despairing laughter wrenched at Wentworth's chest. There was a mad shrillness in it. He went limp; his head rolled laxly....

CHAPTER 3
THE LION MAN'S PLOT

B EYOND THE closed door, in the room next to where Wentworth swooned with pain, the Lion Man sat at ease in a cushioned chair. Against the far wall, Ram Singh lay unconscious, bound hand and foot. But the Lion Man was not looking at him. He was looking at a girl roped snugly to a chair. Both arms were free and one gunman held each. The third stood on guard at the outer door, revolver in hand.

Anger blazed in the girl's dark eyes. Her blue-black hair tumbled in curls about her head and color burned high in her olive cheeks. The ropes cut cruelly into her breasts.

"What have you done with Bud?" she demanded fiercely.

The Lion Man smiled at her lazily. "By Bud, I presume, you mean Brandon Early?" he asked softly. "Mr. Early is my associate. I came here to find certain papers and I discover that you have removed them."

"You lie!" the girl exclaimed vehemently, her head high with courage. "You lie! Bud Early would never have a hand in your crimes! I removed those papers because he told me to do it if he ever disappeared for more than twenty-four hours. I did just what he said."

The girl was impetuous, full of fire. Her black eyes snapped as she defended Brandon Early, but the Lion Man only looked at her sleepily. He lifted one of his hands—the fingers still curled in upon themselves so that it seemed a digitless paw—and brushed a coarse lock of hair back behind his right ear.

"Yes, yes," he agreed smoothly, "but I have brought you a note from Mr. Early."

"You tortured it out of him!" The girl was straining forward against the ropes. She wore a blue suit of knit wool. Through the open-work of the sweater, the red welts from the ropes could be seen on her white skin.

The Lion Man leaned forward also, resting a forearm across his knee. "Don't force me to torture it out of you!" His voice was no longer lazy. It was suddenly harsh and snarling. "We've killed one fool tonight before he would tell us that you had the papers."

The girl gasped. Color fled from her cheeks. "What do you mean?" she whispered.

RICHARD WENTWORTH

The Lion face smiled. "Not your Bud," he murmured softly. "His father!"

"Oh, good Lord! No!" The girl shuddered and her head sagged.

"Will you talk now?" the Lion Man insisted gently, "or will we be forced to kill you as well as Early's father? Slowly, of course. Very slowly." He drawled the last words as if enjoying their sound.

The girl's head snapped up. Her eyes were wide with horror,

but the set of her red lips was firm. "You can kill me," she spoke slowly, "but I won't tell!"

If Wentworth, bound helpless in the next room, could have heard, he would have applauded her courage.

The Lion Man rose to his feet with a mere tensing of his thighs. No hands upon the chair arms helped him. "You asked for it!" he said sharply. He signaled to the two men beside the girl. One stepped in front of her and stood on her feet with his whole weight. Now it was clear why her arms had not been bound to her sides by the rope. The second man leaned forward across her shoulders and caught both wrists. He pulled her arms straight upward.

THE GIRL fought, wrenching violently, but the chair was heavy and the weight of the man on her feet hindered her. Her arms were twisted over the chair back and the torturer began to put his weight of them. The girl's back arched. The ropes bit more deeply into her breasts and held her tight against the chair. Her shoulders bulged. Pain twisted her face. "Oh, God!" she panted out.

"Will you talk now?" the Lion Man paired gently.

"*No!*"

Her shoulder joints popped. She groaned. The gunmen who held her were panting. The one on guard watched her with wet, bright eyes. He licked his lips nervously. The man who stood on her feet clamped a hand on each of her thighs, leaned against her to counterbalance the weight on her arms.

"Where are the papers?" the maned man asked again. The question was drawled, lazy.

"*No!*"

"If he pulls a few more inches," the smooth voice warned gently, "your arms will be permanently crippled."

"No! No! *Ahh-h-h-h!*" The agonized scream was torn from her. Her head lolled and the Lion Man swore.

"She's fainted! Hold it till she recovers," he ordered harshly.

The two men slowly released their holds on the girl, reluctantly stepped back. Their eyes remained fixed upon her greedily. The throat of her sweater had been torn open under the strain. Her skirts had pulled up.

"Leave her alone boys, for the present," the Lion Man repeated.

The two men jerked at his soft voice. They turned away from the girl.

"What next, Chief?" one of them asked. He was the man who had stood on the girl's feet. He had a loose-lipped mouth, a lax face stamped with cowardly baseness. He was hollow-chested.

"I object to that 'chief,'" the Lion Man drawled.

"What next, Aronk Dong?" the loose lips spoke hurriedly, quivering with a spasm of fright.

The leonine head nodded under its weight of coarse hair. Aronk Dong sank down again into his cushioned chair. The room was a modest living-room: a davenport and chairs before an open fireplace that was flanked on either side by book-packed shelves. There were convenient reading lamps about the room, a scholar's home.

"There is not yet money enough," Aronk Dong spoke, "to carry on the work. Tomorrow night we will rob the Central Savings Bank...." As the three men sucked in their breath in surprise, he frowned, vertical creases furrowed between his eyes. "There is no need to be alarmed," he explained. "It will be quite safe, even if it's the richest bank in the city. That's why I chose it. I shall be nearby while you work and at the first hint of interference, I shall loose my lightning upon the police."

"Cheez, ch—Aronk Dong," the loose-lipped one breathed. "That lightning sure is the berries. Does everybody know how to use it up there on Mars where you come from?"

A faint smile stirred the Lion Man's cruel mouth. "No," he said softly. "Even on Mars, everyone does not know the secret. It is reserved for a very few—for the sons of princes, like myself. It was given to me to conquer the earth for our glorious king...." He leaned forward in his chair, fixing the three men with his magnetic, madman's eyes. "And when we have laid low earthly cities and men with my lightning; when we have conquered this globe and claimed it for Mars—you men shall all become counts and dukes!"

"Cheez!" the lax-faced torturer said again. "It sounds too good to be true. I never will forget the time you first told us about it, and…" He shuddered suddenly.

"You are recalling," Aronk Dong murmured softly, "what I did to the man who laughed and called me a liar."

The man nodded mutely, with another shudder.

"We are the race of lions," Aronk Dong purred. "It is not wise to cross us. We are evolved differently than the men of earth. Here, you evolved from the foolish, gibbering apes. On Mars, the feline race rules—the ultimate in the evolution of what you call cats. We are without your foolish, apish traits. We are wise. With us, women are simply females for our pleasure. We are without mercy, and we are… quick to anger!"

HE SPRANG up and the three men shrank back, throwing up protecting arms. Aronk Dong laughed lustily: "I am pleased with you—now," he said. "Let's see if the girl will talk, now."

He crossed to her in a long, gliding stride, seized her black hair in his fist. He yanked up the lolling head and a low moan squeezed from the girl's lips.

"Will you talk?" the Lion Man snarled, "or shall we work on your arms again?" His other hand dropped to her shoulder; his fingers bit into the tortured joint.

The girl's lips trembled. Tears squeezed out of her eyes, but she forced herself to gaze directly into the Lion Man's cruel, narrow stare. She drew a deep breath. "I will not talk," she said clearly.

With an oath, Aronk Dong punched her heavily on the chest. She winced and her eyes sparkled with hatred and scorn.

"Get busy!" the Lion Man commanded his two torturers

to their work. Once more the man stepped on her feet, slowly, heavily with his heels. He crouched before her, slid his hands under her thighs for balance, leering into her blanched face. He leaned out and the second man reached over for her wrists. She tried to evade him, but her arms moved slowly and her face whitened with pain.

"They'll twist your arms off if you don't talk," Aronk Dong growled sharply. "I'm giving you a last chance. My patience is getting very short!"

Tears were sliding down the girl's pale cheeks. Her teeth set in her lip as her arms were pulled up and back slowly. "No," she gasped in agony. "No! Not if you kill me!"

The guard standing against the wall stared fascinated. He did not see the swing-door across the room—the door that led to the kitchen—open slowly. He did not see a bloody hand thrust an automatic through the slit. The automatic jerked with a shot and the man who had been wrenching the girl's arms dropped to the floor with a bullet-hole in the side of his head.

It was then that the guard snapped up his gun—and took a bullet through his heart! The door swung wide, and Wentworth, a snarling grin upon his thin lips, braced his shoulders against the wall.

"Won't someone else reach for his gun, please?" he asked, his voice rasping. "I have more bullets to plough through your putrid flesh!"

CHAPTER 4
THE FIEND'S LIGHTNING

WENTWORTH WAS scarcely able to support his weight as he leaned against the wall. Blood still seeped slowly from his clawed shoulder. His staring eyes were filled with hot lights. His hands were red, but the fist that gripped the automatic, low against his side, did not waver.

The Lion Man and the gangster stared at him incredulously for a half minute, then, Aronk Dong laughed. "Walk over and take that gun out of his hand, Smoker," he commanded his henchman. "He's too weak to pull the trigger."

Wentworth did not speak, but his automatic did. A bullet burned past the gunman's face. The hood stopped, flat on his heels.

"Untie the girl," Wentworth ordered harshly, "or the next bullet will spatter whatever brains you have. Leo, keep your hands still."

"My name is Aronk Dong," the Lion Man objected gently. "I wish you would call me by it." He paused as if thinking. "Permit me to compliment you on your clever escape. It was a remarkable feat."

Wentworth knew that Aronk Dong was playing for time even as the Spider, a short while before, had himself stalled to escape death. But he doubted if the shooting inside the house would bring men from the woods. The other henchmen would be expecting the Spider's execution. Wentworth felt lightheaded; his chest labored with a fearful weakness. He could not gulp enough air into his lungs. He recognized that it was the suffocation which comes from excessive bleeding. His heart was pounding with lightning beats, sending his depleted blood racing through his veins. But it could not appease that awful air-hunger that made the world dim before his eyes.

Through the weakness-haze, he made out that the girl's ropes had fallen away. She rose weakly from the chair and stumbled toward him. "No," he cried hoarsely. "No! Free the man against the wall. Ram Singh."

He saw the girl hazily as she moved toward the Hindu, saw the calm smile on the Lion Man's face. Damn him, Aronk Dong knew how weak he was—knew that within moments, his strength would fail him and the automatic would drop from his hand. The maned man needed no other weapon than time.

"Yes, you were very clever," Aronk Dong whispered. "Tell me how you escaped the ropes."

Wentworth told himself it would do no harm to talk. It might clear his head, help him cling to what little consciousness remained to him. He fastened his gaze on the Lion Man. He saw the other gunman make a swift, furtive movement and he fired twice, deliberately. The automatic almost wrenched from his weakened hand, but the two bullets sped true and the second torturer sprawled twitching on the floor.

"I can still shoot, Aronk Dong," Wentworth said, his voice a dry croak in his throat.

"Quite," the Lion Man agreed. "But you haven't told me yet how you escaped the ropes."

Wentworth knew Aronk Dong was stalling but he was playing for time, too, trying to cling to consciousness until the girl could free Ram Singh. Her arms were filled with the pain of torture; her fingers were clumsy with the knots.

"A simple matter," Wentworth croaked. It was labor to articulate. He needed all that air for his panting lungs. "Simple. Wet rope stretches."

"Wet rope?" The Lion Man was polite. "I do not understand."

Wentworth laughed suddenly, lightheaded. His voice cracked. "Blood has a large water content, Aronk Dong. Blood wet the ropes and they stretched enough to free me. My own blood and that of the man you killed." He laughed again, shrilly, and then checked himself suddenly.

By God, the lights were going out! Aronk Dong was doing something to the lights with his trained lightnings. But the Spider still could shoot… The gun bucked in Wentworth's hand, blasting twice. He felt sharp pain as his shoulder scraped against the wall. Hell, he was falling… falling….

THERE WAS a long black darkness punctuated by flashes of light and blasts of sound. That was followed by hours of awful air-hunger. It racked him with nausea. His lungs were starving. He breathed with his mouth wide open, but even that did not satisfy his blood-drained body. Presently that dreamy scene faded, and when light began to filter into his brain again, his hunger for air had been appeased. The gasping horror was gone. He heard a woman laugh softly and he recognized a voice that called him gently.

"Dick! Oh, Dick!" It was not laughter. It was sobs. Nita, his

Nita, was crying. But his mind was weary. The darkness came back quickly once more....

When he regained consciousness the second time, he found Nita beside him, clasping his one free hand tightly. His left hand was laced snugly against his chest with bandages. Nita was smiling—her violet eyes deep, her lips tender. A shaft of sunlight made a glorious spun bronze halo about her chestnut curls. He was in a hospital room.

It was two days before he could learn what had happened at Brandon Early's isolated cottage, where the Lion Man—Wentworth frowned with bewilderment at the thought of the creature who called himself Aronk Dong—had nearly torn the life from him, as he had killed his gangster underling, with his feline claws.

"Tell me, Nita," Wentworth touched his bandaged shoulder, "what was this wound like?"

Nita paled and the smile left her lips. "It was horrible! Claws, the doctor said, or a claw, had ripped it."

Wentworth nodded. Then it was true, what he remembered—that creature who called himself a Lion Man of Mars. He laughed sharply. "I have the queerest memories," he muttered. "A man with a face like a lion and a mane all red and black; with claws on each hand with which he could kill. A man who claimed to bring devastating man-made lightning from Mars—where they never have lightning because the air is too thin for clouds of any kind, much less storms!"

A puzzled frown disturbed Nita's smooth brows. "Ram Singh says, the same thing," she whispered. "Kirkpatrick was puzzled,

There was a dazzling flash of blue-white flame as the lightning hit the building.

but your delirious account and Ram Singh's statements were exactly alike. The newspapers took Kirk's attitude, but some of them were rather humorous." She smiled slightly.

Kirkpatrick was Commissioner of police, an intimate friend of Richard Wentworth, but a dangerous foe of the Spider.

"If proof that you are the Spider ever falls into my hands, Dick, I shall prosecute you to the full extent of my power," Kirkpatrick had told Wentworth. "But until it does, we will work together for the suppression of crime. I rather admire the swift justice this Spider executes!"

Yes, Kirkpatrick knew Wentworth was the Spider. Even Jackson's false dying confession, when that loyal servant had sacrificed himself for Wentworth a month before, had not altered that. It was a game, a deadly game in which one man's life and another man's honor were at stake.

Wentworth's eyes narrowed suddenly as he recalled the dead gunman in that lonely cottage in the wood. He had died with the Spider's brand on his forehead. Wentworth had been in the cottage in the disguise of the Spider, yet Nita had made no mention of all this…. Even with the pallor of illness on his face, Wentworth was an extraordinary vital man as he lay there in the hospital bed. The stimulation of his thoughts sent color pumping into his cheeks, sharpened his blue-gray eyes to keenness. There was a harsh set of his mobile lips that betrayed the grimness of his thoughts.

"What happened in the cottage?" he asked quietly.

"You shot out the lights," Nita told him, "just as the girl finally got Ram Singh untied. Ram Singh got a gun off the floor and started shooting. He heard the Lion Man yelling for his men. So he mounted guard over the windows. There were plenty of weapons, ammunition and dead men's guns scattered over the floor. The girl slipped out to get help. When police finally smashed in, they found Ram Singh trying to revive you. Apparently you fainted from loss of blood just as you shot out the lights."

"Ram Singh removed my disguise?" Wentworth asked, with a lifting surge of heartbeats for the Hindu's keen judgment.

Nita nodded. "Yes. And the girl was Bets Decker, Brandon Early's secretary. She got only a hazy look at you in the doorway, and you were pretty bloody. She didn't know that the disguise had been removed."

WENTWORTH'S MUSCLES jerked in a start and he winced with a twinge of pain from his shoulder. "But the dead gangster! The one with his face and throat clawed by the Lion Man! Didn't he have a Spider seal on his forehead?"

Nita shuddered, closing her eyes. "He didn't have any forehead," she said in a muffled voice. "Ram Singh thought it best to remove—that, too!"

"Nita!" Wentworth grasped her hand. "Nita! You were there too! You came to that cottage." The realization was more important at the moment than the fact that the Spider was still—officially—dead—cleared by Jackson's heroic gesture.

Nita admitted her presence in the cottage with a little smile. "Ram Singh phoned me. They said here at the hospital that you hadn't long to live, but I convinced them that was silly. You just lost a little blood and transfusions took care of that."

"Transfusions?" Wentworth questioned grimly. "How many?"

The smile hovered about Nita's lips. "Four," she said.

Wentworth's hand tightened about her arm, and she winced. He saw, then, that there was a bandage about the crook of her left elbow. Nita had been one of the four to give her blood.

She answered his swift question as to when it had happened. "In Early's cottage you were dying. I made the doctor take a chance that our blood was the same. It had to be!"

There was a certain low fierceness in Nita's voice, and Wentworth closed his eyes on the tears that stung them. They were not tears for her bravery. Courage between them, in behalf of each other, was no new thing. But an overwhelming bitterness surged up within him.

It was a rare thing that the pain over their self-denial flooded over him, but he was weak now with his wounds. Their only happiness was that they two could fight for each other, side by side. It seemed to Wentworth, lying with his eyes closed, his face grimmer than even he knew, that all the happiness he had ever faced had been when wounds had laid him low and he and Nita tad known a few brief days of companionship—in hospitals—before he had to pick up the struggle again.

For marriage could not be for the Spider, however hotly burned his love. What man could marry with disgrace hanging like a guillotine knife above him? Any hour might find the heavy hand of the law on his shoulder, leading him away to a shameful death. Nita would have been willing to face even that peril, he knew, but if there were children….

He shut his mind rigidly against his bitterness, drove the grimness from his face and opened his eyes, keen and piercing, looking at Nita. He blew out a slow breath, squeezed her hand again. "Has anything more been heard of this man with claws?" Wentworth asked quietly.

Nita shook her head slowly. "You have had enough excitement for the day," she said. "To sleep with you!"

Wentworth shook his head quietly. He knew the reason for the quick fear that crept into Nita's eyes. The Lion Man, Aronk Dong, had struck again with his lightnings. Nita feared that if he learned about the man's activities, he would drive his weakened body from the bed and into the battle.

"You might as well tell me dear," he told Nita with tight-pressed lips. "I won't be foolish about it. I'll get my strength first. I'll have to—that man is not human…" He paused as he realized what he had said. Not human! But of course Aronk Dong was human. Those claws, that lion face, was a simple fake. His ferocity was not greater than the Spider had found before in criminal leaders. A sudden memory struck him.

"The Central Savings Bank!" he cried. "They were going to rob it! After I got my hands free, I waited outside the door, gathering my strength, waiting until the men were too occupied to notice my presence. I heard them plot to rob the Central Savings Bank!"

"They did it, too," Nita told him. "Ram Singh overheard the plot also and warned Kirkpatrick, but the police guard did no good. Lightnings smashed their cars, burned the men to a crisp. The thieves got away with over a quarter of a million dollars."

A violent oath tore from Wentworth's throat. He started

upright in the bed; then sagged back, overwhelmed with weakness, lungs panting.

"You promised, Dick!" Nita was on her feet, hands pressing against his chest. "You promised you would gather your strength before you did anything!"

Wentworth lay supine and gasped, nodding his head weakly. He swallowed, and his voice was faint.

"I'm even weaker than I thought," he said heavily, reluctantly. "I'll have to wait."

TEN DAYS he waited, rebuilding his weakened body, healing the torn muscles of his shoulder. And while he waited, Aronk Dong's lightnings struck wantonly over the country. Strikers marching on a textile factory in North Carolina were blasted into instant, smoky death by a bolt. The judgment of the Lord, a local preacher called it, upholding the benevolence of the capitalist who largely financed his church.

Across the Mississippi, a railway tram was wrecked when a thunderbolt crashed into the cabin of the locomotive, killing both men of the crew. A factory in Yonkers, split asunder under a terrific electrical assault, was swept by flames. Papers spoke of the rising loss from electric storms, and a scientist wrote learnedly on the cycles of the sunspots.

One newspaper hazarded a shrewd guess that the lightnings were artificial and cited facts to prove it. This was the same newspaper that had earlier hired men and offered rewards for the capture or death of the Spider. And now it bewailed the fact that there were not more men like the Spider—that he could not come back to life to battle this new menace against humanity! Only the Spider, the paper went on, would be keen enough to recognize that this was crime and to strike at its base.

A bitter smile twisted Wentworth's mouth as he read this praise from the fickle press. One day baying for his death, the next bemoaning that it had occurred.

Commissioner of Police Kirkpatrick frowned at the paper when it was shown to him. "That's shrewd," he said, "but probably backed more by a desire for sensationalism than conviction that the lightnings are operated by criminals. I haven't dared to tell the theory that you hold. They would only laugh. The people would become panic-stricken!"

Newspapers and radio reports brought news of the panics thunder storms brought wherever they now struck. People went out from their homes into the open, fearfully, crouched miserably in the middle of level fields, far from any tree. Newspapers had told them this was the only safe spot. In the mid-west, they sought old-fashioned cyclone cellars. And still the lightning toll continued.

Everywhere throughout the country, wherever thunder storms swept, the dread lightning struck. The dead were over two hundred. The property damage was incredible. The strange part of the situation was the wanton purposelessness of it all. There seemed absolutely no motive for the carnage and destruction. It was exactly as if some mad storm-god was slaying and ruining on every head in a fit of unreasoning rage.

Finally the day came when Wentworth was permitted to leave the hospital. Nita came for him, but there were the usual delays. After a half hour of impatient waiting, Wentworth was ensconced in the cushioned rear seat of his Lancia town-car, and with Ram Singh at the wheel, was driven off toward his home, The sky was dark with towering nimbus clouds, black and threatening. Against their grim surfaces played the blue-white dance of lightning. Jagged forks of fire quivered and shook and were gone again.

As they wheeled smoothly along the street, Wentworth peered out at the white-faced crowds thronging the sidewalks. These men and women could not take refuge in flat, open fields from the terror of the lightning. They were trapped in the narrow chasms between the high towers of buildings, towers that would surely draw the dread lightnings they feared.

WENTWORTH RECALLED the Lion Man's threat, speaking of these gunmen now dead from the Spider's gun-fire. He was going to conquer the world, he said, and annex it to Mars! Wentworth had laughed then. A stiff smile still stirred his lips at the thought. Foolish, of course, but what was the motive behind this horror?

He scarcely controlled a jerk of his muscles as a thunder clap split the air.

"That was near!" he muttered. Nita was gripping his right arm.

"It was very close," she agreed, and there was strain in her voice. On the sidewalks, men and women broke into frantic, directionless flight. Some ran to the shelter of doorways. Others ducked, rat-like, into the burrows of the subways.

The car pushed on. Wentworth frowned at the turmoil of the streets. A high wind was sweeping through the city canyons; whirling scraps of paper and clouds of dust into the air.

The Lancia droned on down Fifth Avenue. The wind hissed and howled about them. When they were still two blocks from Wentworth's apartment, the first, scattered, heavy drops of rain pelted down.

Wentworth leaned forward to stare at the steadily darkening heavens. He watched a newspaper swirl upward in the grasp of the wind and suddenly his eyes tightened. A queer chill raced along his spine. He lifted his right arm and pointed. "What do you make of that?" he asked in a strange, tight voice.

Nita stared where he directed, then her gaze jerked to his quickly. "Why, it's a balloon!"

Wentworth nodded grimly. He signaled Ram Singh to the curb, climbed out to inspect the bag more closely. Big, wet drops splashed coldly into his upturned face. A boy with a frightened, dirty face scuttled past. The queer chill that had quivered over Wentworth persisted. But now his tense arms felt cold, too.

It was foolish, he told himself. This was just a captive balloon that had broken loose. One of those smaller bags that were sometimes used to float advertisements. It was obvious that it was too small for a passenger craft. He realized that the wind would sweep it directly over his own apartment building. With an abrupt cry, he swung about and sprang to the car.

"Drive to the apartment! Quick!"

Nita's hand gripped his arm as he dropped into the seat. "What is it Dick?" Dread quivered in her voice.

Wentworth sat tensely on the edge of his seat, staring ahead. A curse rasped in his throat as he saw a black limousine slide up in front of the apartment house.

"Kirkpatrick!" he snapped. "Ram Singh, blow that horn and keep it going!"

"What is it, Dick?" Nita demanded again, urgently.

Wentworth shook his head. "I'm not sure, but I can't understand why that balloon should be loose and flying so low over the city...."

The trumpet of the Lancia was repeating its four polite notes in unceasing rhythm. Nita, too, had stiffened. Her fingers dug into Wentworth's good arm, her eyes fixed on the balloon. "You mean—" she queried in a low, tense voice. "You mean that balloon may be bringing... *the lightning!*"

Wentworth jerked his head in a vehement nod. "It seems silly," he acknowledged. "A tiny balloon like that couldn't possibly give off an electrical discharge as strong as lightning. Yet I have a strange feeling that...."

THE CAR swerved to the curb on the wrong side of the street and Wentworth flung himself out. He staggered, caught a stanchion that supported the apartment-house canopy. A glance at the sky showed the balloon a scant hundred feet away from the building, traveling fast. Wentworth could see a black thin thread below it, a trailing line.

"Quick, Kirk," Wentworth snapped. "Lightning is going to hit this building. Warn those inside. Get out again fast!"

Kirk-
patrick stared
at his friend's
white, urgent face for
the space of a heartbeat. Then
he spun on his heel and lunged
into the lobby of the building, slapping
both doors wide. "Ring the fire alarm!" he
shouted. "Lightning has hit the building!"

He raced back to the curb again. With a jerk of his
hand, Wentworth motioned him into the Lancia, started to leap
in after him. His eyes glimpsed a boy with newspapers clutched
under his arm. He was darting toward the supposed safety of
the apartment door.

"Drive, Ram Singh!" Wentworth shouted. "Drive fast!"

He slammed the car door, darted after the newsboy. It was

instinctive, rushing to the boy's rescue at the risk of his own life. It was part of that great love of humanity which made Wentworth the Spider. Coldly calculating where his vengeance upon criminals was concerned, he was yet warm-hearted and impulsive in his reactions to humanity.

So he shouted to Ram Singh to race away leaving him to his fate, and he charged into the apartment doorway after the boy. The newsboy, cap cocked crookedly above a dirty face, was cowering against the desk, but with his legs braced belligerently, his back against the wall, and his boy's face screwed up pugna-

ciously. He was frightened, but it would have cost any friend of his a "sock on the snoot" to mention the fact. Wentworth loved gritty kids like that.

He darted to the boy, throwing a swift glance around the lobby as he did so. The fire-alarm gong was clamoring noisily, the elevators flashing up and down.

"Get out of here, quick, son!" he told the boy. "This building…."

"Make me!" the boy challenged. He ducked to one side, but even his street-gamin' speed was not equal to the split-second movement of the Spider's trained muscles. His right arm shot out and encircled the boy. With the same motion, he whirled and darted for the door, raced out, and cursed. The Lancia still waited at the curb, the door open. Kirkpatrick and Nita had done this, risked their lives, too, so that Wentworth and the boy might have a quick get-away.

Wentworth flung the boy fighting and writhing into the tonneau. As he leaped in afterward, Ram Singh hurled the car forward. Wentworth twisted to stare at the balloon. Behind him, he heard the boy squawking defiantly: "Say, if youse mugs is kidnapers, youse got the wrong guy!" Two, three, four seconds dragged by….

There was a dazzling blaze of blue-white fire that filled all the world. Wentworth had a stunned feeling that he *heard* of thunder. Ram Singh reeled in his seat, braked to a halt.

Fumbling for the door knob, Wentworth thrust out into the street and stared behind him, wrenched his gaze up to the apartment building. The balloon had vanished. Rain was pouring down in cascades, but a shimmer of blue-white fire still played over the apartment building. From its roof downward for half of its fifteen-story height, a great gaping crack had been rent in the bricks!

Even as he watched, the crack widened, the wall swayed outward. A few separate bricks became detached and whipped away. Then with an appalling lack of sound, the entire wall crumpled. It smashed downward, disintegrating, shredding fragments and dust far and wide like a violently-hurled shovelful of ashes. The mass of debris struck—half upon a terraced projection five stories above the street and half in the street itself. An automobile roaring past that instant was smashed to oblivion and rocketed, wrecked, against the wall. Then came the sound of the destruction, a rumbling echo of that fearful crash of thunder. It beat upon deadened ear-drums.

Dust puffed upward, rolled along the earth and was battered down once more by the rain. Up toward the roof, seven stories of apartments were open to rain and wind and storm. Floors sagged. Gaunt skeleton ribs of steal were exposed. It was strangely like a doll-house with a removable side. But there was nothing small or insignificant about the disaster. In one of those exposed rooms, a davenport stood on a sagging floor. On it was all that was left of what had once been a human being. The corpse was charred and black.

Wentworth sagged back weakly, caught at the side of his car. Then he lurched forward toward his apartment building. He owned the entire structure, had purchased it as an additional protection against his underworld enemies so that he could build up his defenses. But it was not the financial loss that staggered Wentworth. It was the countless men and women who had died.

His previous doubts about the man-made lightning were wiped out now. He had only guessed that the floating balloon was part of the mechanics of the blast, but he had been terribly right. A sudden thought struck him. Jenkyns, old Jenkyns, his faithful butler for many years, and his father's servant before him, had been in the apartment!

He broke into a heavy run, unaware of the rain that drenched him, ignoring the burning ache of his wounded shoulder... He realized now that this lightning blast had been no accident. The blow had been aimed at him directly, at the Spider! It had been intended to destroy him, and only his chance delay at the hospital had saved him.

Wentworth was certain, all at once, that none of the lightning blasts had been without a purpose. Behind them all was a deliberate, deadly purpose that meant money for that criminal monster who called himself Aronk Dong, the Lion Man of Mars!

CHAPTER 5
"EARL OF THE ELECTRONS"

WENTWORTH SWUNG into the lobby of his apartment building, panting terribly from weakness and exertion. He pulled to a short stop. A white-haired old man, whose usually ruddy, cheerful face was pale and drawn with worry, tottered toward him with outstretched hands. "Master Dick! Master Dick!" he cried. "Thank God you're safe!"

Wentworth put out an uncertain hand and braced it against the wall. "It's good to see you, too, Jenkyns," he said quietly. "I thought you might be upstairs." He swung toward the uniformed hall-boys. "Get everyone out of the building at once and call engineers for an inspection."

He turned back toward the door. "Jenkyns, shift my things to the Ritz-Carlton and engage a suite. I'll be there later."

Kirkpatrick came pounding in at a dead run, his face stern as ribbed rock. Fire and police sirens mingled on the streets. An excited crowd was already gathering about the doors. Wentworth heard the newsboy's shrill insolent voice outside.

"Me for this," he piped. "Lightning never strikes twice in the same place."

Wentworth's mouth twisted. He conjectured that the lightning would strike at him again, twice, a hundred times! Kirkpatrick took him by the arm, his faultless clothing awry for once, drenched by rain. Even the dampness of his spike-end mustache was gone.

"Come along, old man," he urged. "There's nothing we can do here, and that wetting won't do you any good, just out of the hospital as you are."

The Lancia was waiting at the door and Nita gestured imperatively. Wentworth strode toward the car, his face hard with determination. He stopped abruptly when the newsboy, his cap still cocky, stepped into his path.

"Say, mister," he piped shrilly, "that was swell, yanking me out of that building. Thanks a lot." He stared up into Wentworth's face, completely serious. "But I'll bet you can't catch me again easy as that."

Wentworth snatched at him, grinning, but the boy was gone in a twinkling, jeering from the middle of the street. Wentworth climbed into the Lancia and there was a lingering smile about his mouth corners that was tribute to the gamin's dexterity. He spoke rapidly to Kirkpatrick.

"Listen, Kirk, that balloon couldn't have been released very far away. The wind wouldn't carry it straight to this spot if it were. It must have been released…" He stopped, stared downward and pointed toward a tall apartment building on the opposite side of the street and two blocks away. "The balloon came from there!" He was suddenly excited. His voice crackled with decision. He sprang to the car, snapped a brisk order at Ram Singh.

"You're going straight to my apartment, Dick," Nita objected. "You're wet to the skin."

Wentworth reached out and squeezed her hand. "In a few moments, darling," he promised her. His voice was alert and vital. That long siege in the hospital, the slow days of recuperation, were wiped out in an instant by his sharply aroused energies.

"But, Dick," Kirkpatrick's dipped accents were grave. "You aren't even sure that balloon had anything to do with the lightning."

Wentworth laughed sharply, his eyes on the entrance of the apartment building toward which they drove through the rain. "If I see an object pointed at me and right after that, a bullet hits me," he said, "I deduce that the object fired the shot even if I don't see the bullet or think the object looks like a gun."

KIRKPATRICK LOOKED at his friend's sharply chiseled, dynamic profile. He recognized that words were futile. Wentworth had set a goal.

First out when the car halted, Wentworth pounded into the apartment building. His weakness had dropped from him and his step was aggressive. "The north penthouse," Wentworth snapped at the man behind the ball desk. "Who occupies it?"

The man raised polite eyebrows. His eyes swept Wentworth's wet, bedraggled clothing, then rose to his face. There was a faint disdain about his small, flexible lips, but when he met Wentworth's eyes, he jerked as if he had received a galvanic shock. "The north penthouse, sir," he said politely, "is empty."

Wentworth uttered an exclamation of triumph. "Take us up there immediately!"

The clerk hesitated only a moment. He came out from behind the desk and revealed himself in formal cut-away coat and morning trousers. He bowed respectfully, gestured toward an elevator door.

"Ah, Dick!" Kirkpatrick murmured in Wentworth's ear, "if only I could command such immediate obedience without even showing a police badge!"

Wentworth grinned. "Nonsense, Kirk," he said. Weakness plucked suddenly at the backs of his knees. A dull throbbing gnawed at his left shoulder, but pains faded away in the heat of the chase. That it was a chase, Wentworth was positive. This building was the only one from which the balloon could have come, and the penthouse on the north side was the sole spot from which such a balloon, trailing a line, could be released without attracting attention. And now he found that penthouse was supposed to be untenanted!

He lifted his right hand, touched the automatic that nestled beneath his left arm. It had been painful to strap the holster in place over the claw-torn shoulder, but he had insisted upon it.

At the top floor, the clerk stepped aside for them to leave the elevator. "Stay in the elevator and give me the key," Wentworth ordered.

Once more the man hesitated. "You have authority, sir?" he asked fearfully, apologetically. "This might involve me with the owners, and…."

"I am Police Commissioner Kirkpatrick," Kirkpatrick's quiet, clipped voice affirmed and the man capitulated without a further word.

Wentworth was never more cheerful than when on a man-hunt trail. He opened the penthouse door and shouldered in with a gun in his hand. The dim, reflected light of the overcast sky showed a large, empty room with French doors that opened onto the terrace. These had been flung wide and the dwindling rain blew in on polished hardwood floors.

All these things Wentworth saw in a glance, but his gaze centered upon a man who stood in the middle of the room. He was built like a heavyweight champion with a ruff of golden yellow hair that hung awry across his forehead. Rimless glasses perched upon his nose. He was staring down at a collection of gas cylinders on the floor. At Wentworth's abrupt entrance he looked up with mild, near-sighted eyes. He blinked at the leveled gun, looked over at Kirkpatrick. Then his fists clenched at his sides, his shoulders rocked forward. He strode toward them with a belligerence that contrasted ridiculously with his mild *pince-nez* stare.

"Drat it!" he boomed in a loud, deep voice. "Drat it. I've had enough of this!" His words were pettish, almost fretful. "I've had enough! Put aside those silly guns or I'll… I'll." He shook his two fists. They were huge and knotted.

WENTWORTH FROWNED, but he poised his gun warily in his hand. A clever man was behind all these crimes, and he did not intend to be tricked into laxness.

"Just who are you?" Wentworth queried quietly. "And what are you doing in this apartment?"

"I am Brandon Early," the man's booming, but nevertheless pettish voice stated. "I came to this apartment to recover some experimental apparatus."

A startled curse sounded behind Wentworth. Kirkpatrick stepped forward. "You are under arrest, Mr. Early," he said grimly in his sharp, clipped voice.

"Under arrest? Under arrest!" Early shook his fists again. "I've had enough of this foolishness, I tell you…" He started toward Wentworth. Kirkpatrick sprang to meet Early and received a solid blow to the jaw. He reeled backward, attempted a counter-punch. Brandon Early, for all his mild manner, evaded the blow easily and stepped forward again. Kirkpatrick took Early's fist on the jaw again and went down.

Brandon Early threw back his head and laughed deep booming laughter. He hunched his shoulders forward, blond hair sprawling across his forehead, and came toward Wentworth again. His eyes gleamed angrily behind the rimless glasses.

Wentworth shook his head in a puzzled way and put his automatic back in its under-arm holster.

"Just a minute, Bud," he spoke calmly. "I'm the man who kept Bets Decker from being tortured. I'd like to talk with you for a few minutes."

At the name of the girl, the man stopped uncertainly. "Then you're not a gangster?" he asked in disappointment.

Wentworth stared at Early in bewilderment. This was the man who, in his own mind, he blamed for all the murders and destruction that had been caused by chained lightning. Yet the man was either putting over the best pretense of innocence he had ever beheld, or else he was actually without guilt. Wentworth felt suddenly weak. A hint of nausea gnawed at the pit of his stomach. He was still too sick for these exertions. He put his shoulders against the wall, peering at the blond young giant before him—at the blue and puzzled eyes behind the glasses.

"You just knocked out Police Commissioner Kirkpatrick," Wentworth said. He frowned, irritated at the weakness of his voice. "You'd better revive him, and while you do it, you'd better figure out a damned good reason for being here!"

"The Police Commissioner! Oh, my goodness gracious!" The words sounded ludicrous in Brandon Early's deeply masculine voice. Wentworth almost laughed—and realized that he was feeling a little light-headed.

"Come on, get busy and revive him!" he ordered.

Early went down on his knees beside Kirkpatrick. With a massage of neck vertebrae as skillful as Wentworth himself could have managed, he revived the Commissioner. He began a hurried, confused apology.

"I thought you were gangsters," he explained. "I've met so many of the vermin recently that the mere sight of a firearm fills me with revulsion."

Kirkpatrick was on his feet now, eyeing Early belligerently. "You don't say!" he growled sarcastically. "And when you revolt, you use your fists, is that it?"

Early nodded at him gravely. "I'm afraid that is frequently the case," he agreed.

Wentworth thrust himself out from the wall, feeling a little giddy. "Kirk, would you mind if we all went up to Nita's to talk this over?"

Kirkpatrick turned to him quickly, concern on his face, and Wentworth realized his voice had been thick.

"Certainly not! Here, Early, lend a hand. Mr. Wentworth is just out of the hospital."

"I shall be glad to go with you gentlemen," Early said amiably, helping Wentworth. "You'll have to permit me to bring my fiancée along, Miss Alice Auruckner. I left her waiting downstairs while I come up here to make an investigation. I had received an anonymous communication that I would find some criminals here this afternoon."

THIS TIME, Wentworth couldn't choke down the laughter that pushed up into his throat.

Early looked at him strangely, eyes bright. "Really, I was quite provoked to find the criminals gone," he said. "However, they did leave behind a bit of equipment. And I have a clue to their identity also."

Wentworth halted in the walk from the elevator to the street. "And what is that?" he asked in a voice he tried to make quiet.

"I found some hairs there which I am quite sure…" Early hesitated, nodded to himself. "Yes, I am quite positive they belonged to Aronk Dong, the Lion Man of Mars!"

The rush of cool air from the street cleared Wentworth's head and he studied the bulky figure of the "Earl of the Electrons." He was youngish, not thirty yet, but his discoveries in the field of science had been little short of miraculous. He was hailed as a new Edison, a genius, this bungling, young man with the body of a prize-ring champion and the pedantic speech of a scholar.

"Permit me to ask," Wentworth fought hard to keep the laughter out of his voice, "do you believe that this gentleman who calls himself Aronk Dong actually came from Mars?"

"Oh, assuredly," Early answered in surprise. "He explained the system that was used: A perfected method of neutralizing gravity was employed to build a ship. That is a thing on which I had hoped to work some day myself."

Wentworth stared at the man hard. Was all this a sham—this odd contrast between body and mind and voice? This absurd credulity? Hell, this man might be the Lion Man himself! He recalled with a shock that the Lion Man had boasted that Early's father already had died under the torture.

"By the way," Wentworth asked quietly, "where is your father?"

Early shook his head, turned a frank and open face that was frowning with worry.

"I've been asking myself that same question for days," he said. "The *pater* disappeared while I was up in the Maine woods doing some experiments, and I haven't seen him since!"

CHAPTER 6
A MACHINE GUN INTERRUPTS

WENTWORTH FROWNED over the information concerning the elder Early's disappearance, recalling what Aronk Dong had said about torture death. It was true that police, searching the cottage, had found no trace of the old man who lived alone with his inventor son. He shrugged it aside. That would have to wait on further details from Early.

On the sidewalk before the apartment house—the rain had now subsided to a slight dirty drizzle—Brandon Early ducked an awkward bow, excusing himself to fetch his fiancée.

"I'll just go along, if you don't mind," Kirkpatrick told him grimly. Early blinked at him and Wentworth thought that he paled a little, but he assented readily enough and the two men swung off together. Kirkpatrick strode with his usual almost military erectness, quick energy in every footfall. Early's pace was more shambling, but not without a heavy, muscular grace. Only his massive head, thrust forward, causing his shoulders to stoop slightly, spoiled his carriage. That might easily be assumed....

Wentworth stood beside his Lancia, the door open, telling

Nita swiftly what had occurred in the penthouse above. In a moment, the two men came back again, bringing a diminutive blonde between them. She was dressed in squirrel fur from pert hat to trim, gray boots. She held a tight, little muff high before her peaches-and-cream face. Above it her blue eyes were slyly roguish and tendrils of straw-colored hair made ringlets about her ears.

"My fiancée," Bud Early said proudly, beaming from behind his thick-lensed glasses. "Miss Alice Auruckner!"

Wentworth completed the introductions and suavely arranged the seating—Early between Nita and the little blonde in the back; himself and Kirkpatrick half-facing them on the kick seats. The rain was soundless now, glossing the asphalt as the day faded. The wet purring of the tires murmured faintly as Ram Singh sent the Lancia smoothly toward Nita's apartment.

"Early," Wentworth began abruptly, "you have perfected a method of creating man-made lightning?"

Early's face registered shock, innocent-seeming, blue eyes widening behind the glasses.

"I didn't know it was…" he stammered. "Yes, I have, but how did you know?"

"How does it operate?" Kirkpatrick demanded.

Early shook his big head, smiled. He had a ridiculously tiny hat high on his head; his blonde hair stubbornly pushed out from under it in wild strands. "You surely don't expect me to tell that, do you, gentlemen?" he asked. "It hasn't been patented yet!"

"Then you're the only person who knows the method?"

Gloom clouded Early's face. "No," he admitted slowly. "Some

of my plans were stolen from me. That's where I've been the last few days—trying to get them back. Criminals...." He broke off with a quick suspicious glance at the two men before him. "How do I know you're what you claim to be?" he demanded suddenly.

His hand darted to his overcoat pocket.

As if he had been expecting that identical move, Wentworth lifted his right hand into view. It held an automatic. "Leave your gun in your pocket, Early," he said decisively.

The blonde girl let out a small, choked squeal of fright. Early turned to her with quick, solicitous hands. "Now, Alice," he said soothingly, "it's quite all right."

"Quite," said Wentworth grimly. "I can easily prove that we are exactly as we represent ourselves to be, but Mr. Early has some explaining to do. It happens that his invention has been used to kill several hundred persons—to destroy millions of dollars worth of property! Furthermore, we have just arrested him on the scene of another lightning attack."

"This is preposterous!" Early cried angrily. "I went up there because someone telephoned me that the men who stole my invention would be there at a certain time."

WENTWORTH LAUGHED. "So you went all by yourself, and never thought of calling the police?"

Early nodded seriously. "Certainly. The person that phoned me said it was necessary to go alone."

"Arrested!" Alice Auruckner said it in a weak, shocked voice. "Oh, I never, never..." She seemed about to faint. Her pink cheeks had gone pale; her eyes were starry, brimming with tears. Wentworth could not help contrasting her with Early's secre-

NITA VAN SLOAN

tary, the valiant Bets Decker, who had withstood torture at the hands of the ruffians rather than reveal her employer's secrets. It took no psychic powers to know that Bets had been motivated by more than loyalty. How could a man overlook such a vivid brave woman and be fascinated by this fainting blonde, Wentworth wondered, watching Early's concern.

"Miss Auruckner is all right," Wentworth said brusquely. "That's enough stalling. Tell us at least the basic underlying principles on which your man-made lightning operates."

Early stared back at him with a rising belligerence, but finally shrugged. "In view of what you have said about the casualties," he said meekly, "I suppose you are quite right in asking. The principle is really quite simple. For ages, people have thought that lightning came from the skies. This was a false impression. I have proved that the main discharge in a lightning flash comes from the earth itself.

"I'm not alone in my discoveries. Two South African scientists—their names wouldn't mean anything to you—perfected a camera with a lens that operated fifteen hundred times a minute, and with that, took marvelously accurate pictures of lightning flashes. They found that only a pale, arrow-shaped flash came from the heavens—a sort of an electron avalanche—which opened a path for the main discharge from the earth. Since the entire thing takes only fifty-five millionths of a second, you can understand why people have been fooled so long."

Wentworth remembered of the blue fire dancing over the hood of his car when he had first encountered the man-made lightning. He recalled the balloon with its single, dangling strand of wire and realized that there was no reason why he should have

suspected so innocent an appearing object. Certainly, it could not have discharged that tremendous bolt which had wrecked his apartment house.

"My invention," Early continued, smiling, "consists of a way of concentrating the static electricity in the earth at any given spot. Then it is touched off by a small discharge from above. Actually, all the discharge from above does is to open a path for the release of the electricity in the earth. A wire carrying a very weak, negative voltage would accomplish the same thing."

It was obvious that Early was completely engrossed in his subject. He leaned forward, pointed a finger into the palm of his hand while he talked.

"You've heard people talk for years about lightning rods getting 'charged up,' to use a vulgar phrase. They were under the impression that this electricity was drawn from the air. It is fairly obvious now that the reverse is true; the rods stored up electrical force from all the surrounding territory: earth, buildings and trees, and discharged this current whenever a leader flash came anywhere near it.

"The reason high spots are said to 'attract' lightning is simply that electricity, static in the earth, tends to reach out toward the heavens from the highest possible point just as if, placing two wires parallel, you then bent them so that some portions were nearer together than others. You would find the current jumping at that point." He leaned back in the seat. "I trust I have made myself clear?"

"Entirely," Kirkpatrick nodded, "except on one point. How do you cause the electricity to gather in one particular point?"

Early wagged a long fore-finger, "Ah, that would be telling," he laughed, almost kittenish.

AN ABRUPT grinding crash jerked Wentworth's gaze to the left. Another car had crunched into the Lancia, driving it to the curb. A man leaned out of the window of the other car with a leveled machine gun, centered on Kirkpatrick and Nita.

"Don't none of youse bat an eye," the man snarled, "or I rubs out the dame and the commissioner foist."

Other men spilled from the car, circled in a rush. Wentworth's quick glance showed that they were in the east drive of Central Park. A few other cars showed their headlights in the deepening dusk, purred past. To them, this was simply a commonplace, minor collision over which the occupants were arguing. The machine gun was carefully shielded by the gangster's body.

Two men jerked open the door beside Wentworth, leveled automatics. Alice Auruckner squealed again, and this time, she really did faint. "Hop down, bozo!" the gunman snarled at Wentworth, and as he reluctantly obeyed, the other one turned to Early.

"Okay, Chief," he said. "Didn't we take them slick?"

Early got out of the limousine. Two men hustled him toward the other car while a third held an automatic leveled on Wentworth and Kirkpatrick, and the machine gun menaced them from behind.

"We got your signal when you came out of the apartment, Chief," one of the men was telling Early, "but this was the first chance we got to do anything about it."

Wentworth heard Early's pettish, booming voice vaguely.

Then the men had gone around to the other side of the limousine, and climbed in. Wentworth was stunned by the smooth efficiency of the maneuver. While Early had engrossed them with his talk of electro-mechanics, the gangsters had rolled alongside to rescue their chief. No longer was there any doubt in his mind of Early's guilt. The car backed clear, the machine gun still menacing Wentworth and Kirkpatrick as it droned away.

"Down!" Wentworth snapped the words to Kirkpatrick and flung himself flat on the slippery, wet grass. They were just in time. The machine gun stuttered angrily from the rear window of the speeding limousine. Buzzing slugs cut the air within inches of their heads. Then the car was gone, and the fusillade was over.

Wentworth sprang up, leaped to the front seat beside Ram Singh. "After them!" he snapped.

The Hindu turned a rage-distorted face. "*Sahib*, I cannot!" he cried. "They shot the tires off the front wheels with the machine gun!"

Kirkpatrick was standing beside the car. Wentworth whirled away, sprang into the roadway to commandeer another car for the chase. Kirkpatrick stopped him.

"It would be suicide to chase that bunch with anything less than an armored car, Dick," he said quietly. "They won't hesitate to use the machine gun."

Wentworth was tense with anger at the trap in which they had been snared.

"It was my fault!" he said bitterly. "If I hadn't suggested we come to Nita's apartment, this couldn't have happened."

"On the contrary," Kirkpatrick disagreed him, "It would have happened even if we had driven to police headquarters. And many men would probably have been killed. Well find Early and his gang all right. We forced him to show his hand and that couldn't have happened if you hadn't led me to that apartment house."

LATER, THEY found out that Kirkpatrick had been wrong about that. While he and Wentworth had been going to the penthouse where they had captured Brandon Early, an anonymous telephone call to police headquarters had revealed that "the man behind the lightnings" was in the apartment. But Kirkpatrick and Wentworth had taken their prisoner away before police cars arrived on the scene.

Wentworth had sent Alice Auruckner home alone in a taxi, Nita had gone in the Lancia. Attired now in dry clothing at police headquarters, Wentworth and Kirkpatrick were skimming over the reports of the day, seeking new clues to the hideaway of the lightning gang, reading with gloomy faces accounts of the destruction wrought by the bolts. This was a frequent thing, this cooperation between Wentworth and Kirkpatrick on major crimes. Kirkpatrick, swift and efficient organizer that he was, had many times taken his friend's advice in battles again the underworld.

It was thus they preferred to work, but there were times when the Spider identified as Wentworth was hunted by police, when evidence pointed to him and forced Kirkpatrick to harry him from furtive hideouts and through long days and nights of flight.

Those were the days when lines of worry and age etched themselves deeply on Kirkpatrick's face—when his stern countenance became drawn and bitter. But he would not swerve from his duty, nor play the coward's role by resigning his post. The two men understood each other completely. Each respected in the other the quality that sometimes made them enemies.

But now they fought side by side. Kirkpatrick looked up with anger flashing in his gray eyes. "Lightning smashed the tracks of the elevated out on the Mercer section," he growled harshly. "A train plunged to the ground; thirty were killed."

Wentworth's throat rasped with a curse, but a shrewd look succeeded the angry one. He leaned forward, tapping a forefinger on the edge of the desk.

"The Mercer division was the section the elevated company wanted to abandon," he observed dryly.

Kirkpatrick frowned. His eyes were questioning.

"The Yonkers factory that was destroyed was on the verge of bankruptcy," Wentworth added softly. "In the west, the railroad that had such a disastrous wreck as a result of lightning was having a bitter fight with another line. It was driving both of them to the wall."

Kirkpatrick's hard brown fist smashed down on the desk. "By God, Dick!" he cried. "I believe you've struck the motive behind these killings!"

He snatched up the reports and thumbed through them hurriedly again, sorting out five. "Three tenement buildings have been wrecked," he read aloud. "A fish market and a cleaning-and-dying plant went up in smoke."

"That last sounds like racketeering," Wentworth mused.

"It's possible!" Kirkpatrick was excited now. "It's certainly possible!"

He punched a button on his desk. A policeman thrust a square, carroty head in at the door, saluting precisely. Kirkpatrick held out the reports. "I want the owner of every one of these buildings brought here," he snapped. "Rush order!"

"Yis, sorr," carrot-top answered with a thick brogue. "Commissioner, there's a gent on the phone says his name is Mark Auruckner."

Kirkpatrick glanced at Wentworth, his fat brows arched in a question. Wentworth's eyes were amused. "That's sweet Alice's papa," he murmured. "Worth about five millions, even by post-depression standards."

"I'm busy," Kirkpatrick clipped. He picked up more reports with a growled curse in his throat.

THE POLICEMAN saluted again, about-faced. His eyes, brushing Wentworth's face, were hostile. Wentworth laughed. There had been a time when expediency had forced him to bend a revolver barrel over that carrot-top, and Kirkpatrick's official secretary apparently could not forgive him.

"How about dinner?" he asked Kirkpatrick. "I foresee a busy evening when these tenement owners and what-not begin to come in."

Kirkpatrick glanced at a wrist-watch, grunted and strode across the room to a wardrobe, where he clapped on a stiff, formal felt. Everything about the commissioner was meticulously correct. He paused to take a gardenia from a slender glass vase on his desk.

Wentworth stood, his eyes narrowed. "Listen, Kirk," he questioned slowly, "isn't Auruckner behind the Discus Steel Company?"

Kirkpatrick studied him, adjusting the gardenia in his lapel without looking at it. "You'd know more about that than I do," he said.

"I think Auruckner is behind Discus," Wentworth continued, still slowly. "And Discus owns that factory up in Yonkers that was destroyed by lightning. Also, if I'm not mistaken, Early is employed in Auruckner's laboratories."

Kirkpatrick's hands hung idle now. He was frowning at Wentworth, his head bent slightly forward, brows down. "You think Auruckner may be involved?"

"Also," Wentworth continued, ignoring the question, "Auruckner has textile holdings, and it's barely possible that those strikers who were killed by lightning were attacking one of his plants."

"You're full of ideas tonight," Kirkpatrick said with a tight smile. He snatched up his phone and ordered an inquiry on the strength of Wentworth's surmises. Going through the outer office, Kirkpatrick told carrot-top: "If Mark Auruckner calls again, I'll see him here at my office in two hours." Then he turned and the two men went on down to the commissioner's car.

"The club?" Wentworth suggested.

Kirkpatrick nodded, gave orders to the chauffeur, then settled back on the cushions. "Now, what's your idea about all this?" he demanded.

Wentworth offered a cigarette, lighted one for himself also before he spoke, his head tilted back against the seat.

"It's not at all clear," he began finally, "but it looks to me as if the man who was manufacturing lightning, probably Early, is hiring himself out to destroy property and lives. There are plenty of companies and individuals in the country not too scrupulous to use such a weapon. Insurance could be collected; rivals put out of running; racketeers could enforce their demands. I predict we'll have more lightning attacks along the Mercer line, until the very people who have been fighting against its removal will demand that it be taken down as a menace to life."

"But where does Auruckner come in?" Kirkpatrick was no longer leaning back. He was hunched forward with forearms on his knees, face tense, as Wentworth studied his profile against the flickering change of street lights.

"Perhaps just as a purchaser of destruction," Wentworth drawled. "I'm not sure. Maybe he is financing the operations. If you recall, there were two bank robberies at the start."

"How about the man from Mars?" Kirkpatrick asked.

"That's humbug," Wentworth exploded, anger rising in his breast. "Absurd humbug!"

They alighted before the club, paced up its broad steps and through the funereal columns at the door. They surrendered hats and canes and sauntered toward the dining room.

"Man from Mars!" Wentworth jeered again. "It's ridiculous on the face of it!"

"Are you certain?"

WENTWORTH AND Kirkpatrick whirled as a laughing

voice made the query just behind them. A man blinked at them owlishly from behind shell-rimmed glasses. Kirkpatrick struck out his hand.

"When did you return from the sticks, Jones?" he demanded. He gestured to Wentworth, introduced him. "This is Horace Jones, who makes his living misleading the people of America!"

Wentworth shook hands. "And that means just what?" he queried.

"I write what are vulgarly known as 'pulp' stories," Horace Jones explained. "Yarns for those magazines with wild and woolly covers. 'City of Corpses.' 'Buckets of Blood' or barrels, it doesn't matter."

Wentworth laughed, then grew serious. "I know a lot of people laugh at those stories," he said, "but there's grave truth in many of them. Criminals are well organized, and all of them aren't fools. I've encountered more than one mad genius among them."

Horace Jones snapped the fingers of a big, well-manicured hand. "I knew I'd heard your name. You're the Spider!"

Wentworth smiled, gestured to Kirkpatrick. "He only knows what he reads in the papers," he complained.

Kirkpatrick was scowling. "Really, Jones," he said seriously, "you ought to be careful how you fling out accusations like that. Wentworth could sue you for your shirt for broadcasting such a statement."

Jones laughed. He was a big, hearty man, without the usual paunch of those who spend most of their lives behind a typewriter. He had well-behaved black hair and a fine set of glisten-ing, white teeth. Behind his glasses, his eyes were merry.

"Sue ahead," he chuckled. "All I've got is a little farm in Connecticut and that's in my wife's name. I was just having dinner. Won't you join me?"

"Coward!" Wentworth laughed, "hiding behind a woman's skirts!"

Kirkpatrick said, "Dinner was our idea, too."

The three men sauntered on into the dining room together, followed a bowing head-waiter to a quiet corner.

"Seriously," Horace Jones took up the conversation again, "what's this Man from Mars stuff? You know I turn out reams of copy on interplanetary ships, fourth dimension and time machines. And I've done a mass of stuff on Mars. Just what were you talking about, if I'm not too inquisitive?"

Kirkpatrick snorted. "You're not inquisitive at all, Jones. You're just being natural. You're a born buttinski!" The commissioner smiled.

Jones lifted an amber brandy-stinger against a small lamp on the table. "It's my early training," he apologized with mock seriousness. "My father was a newspaper man!"

The man's manner was pleasant and polished. His high, knotty forehead was intelligent but Wentworth fought against an instinctive, insistent distaste for which he could find no basis. To be sure, the man's lips were a bit too full for masculine taste— sensual, cherry red. A girl passed the open doorway of the room, escorted toward the ladies' parlor by two attentive men, and Jones' eyes followed her avidly. Wentworth shrugged. He didn't personally like men with that slant, but he was no critic of other men's morals. And the fellow was certainly an entertaining companion. He decided suddenly to tell Jones about the Man from Mars with his reddish mane and his deadly claws. There was a dull, reminiscent throb in his left shoulder. The wetting of the day hadn't helped it.

He could see Jones' imagination take fire as he talked, see his keen eyes brighten. The author's fingers kept twirling the stemmed glass.

"By heaven!" he exclaimed when Wentworth had finished. "There's material there for at least six novels and a couple of dozen short stories thrown in!"

"I'll call around for my commission," Wentworth said dryly. "But seriously, do you accept that creature at his face value?"

HORACE JONES waved his left hand, palm upward. "I can't tell you," he said. "Didn't you believe in him when those claws ripped into your shoulder?"

"The claws were real enough," Wentworth admitted, "but it could all have been faked. The Hindus in the back country have a weapon they call a Tiger's Claw. It is a series of razor-sharp, steel talons that fasten to the hand. They inflict rather horrible wounds with it."

Jones nodded. "There's always a logical explanation for everything," he said. "But why couldn't this be true? A man from Mars, coming in a machine equipped with anti-gravity plates. A race that evolved along different lines than our own. Yes, damn it I do believe it!"

Wentworth and Kirkpatrick laughed, but it was not with

72

complete enjoyment. In the backs of their minds lingered a doubt.

They went on with the dinner. Presently a noisy disturbance took the head-waiter with hurried, skipping steps across the dining-room. Before he could reach the doorway, a girl doubled under a waiter's outstretched arras and raced straight across the room toward where they were sitting.

Wentworth was on his feet instantly, recognizing Bets Decker, Early's courageous young secretary. She had lost her hat in the struggle and her black hair sprawled awry on her head. Her cheeks were red with exertion, and anger flamed in her black eyes.

She came to an imperious stand before Wentworth; head flung back, arms rigid at her sides. "What have you done with Bud?" she demanded fiercely. "You can't fool me by that trick that you pulled in the Park which the papers are giving such a spread. You had him kidnapped so you could question him in secret."

Kirkpatrick was on his feet now. Horace Jones stepped forward and laid a soothing hand on the girl's arm. She jerked free, stepped even closer to Wentworth.

"I warn you, you can't get away with it," she squalled. "I know I owe you something for getting me away from that torturer, but you can't misuse Bud."

The head-waiter came up, his perpetually smiling face looking a little sickish. "I'm sorry, miss," he murmured in Bets' ear. "Ladies aren't allowed in here."

Bets said clearly, emphatically: "Go to hell!"

Wentworth stepped forward, nodded to the head-waiter.

"We're upsetting the digestion of quite a few of the more fossilized club members," he told Bets Decker, taking her arm. "Let's go into the ladies' parlor to talk it over?"

"You're not going to soft-soap me," Bets declared vigorously. But she allowed herself to be led from the room.

Horace Jones kept up an excited deep-voiced babble. "I say," he was eager. "The girl has spunk, you know? And she's pretty as the devil!"

Bets tossed her head, permitted Wentworth to seat her in the lounge.

"Listen, Bets." He looked directly into her angry black eyes. "I swear to you that we don't know where Bud Early is."

She glanced defiantly into his eyes for a moment then, pitifully, her lips began to tremble. "Drat it," she mumbled. "I have to go and pull a waterworks act."

She snatched out a scrap of handkerchief, dabbed at her eyes and lifted her round, firm chin bravery. Her eyes searched Wentworth's deeply and gradually fear crept into them. "I believe you," she whispered. "I have to. But, oh God, what has happened to Bud?"

WHEN SHE left, Jones insisted on escorting her to a hotel, and Kirkpatrick and Wentworth resumed their interrupted dinner. The meal was flat after the excitement and they hurried through it, returned to headquarters to find that Mark Auruckner, five times a millionaire, had been waiting fifteen minutes, not too patiently.

Auruckner bowed stiffly to Kirkpatrick, acknowledged an introduction to Wentworth and stood glaring. He carried himself very erectly, as if in an effort to counter-balance the weight of his paunch, which a tailor had striven manfully, but vainly, to conceal. He had scanty gray hair. His bald pate boasted a faint silvery fuzz, and like his face, was beautifully sun-tanned. Despite his paunch, he had an air of physical alertness. Wentworth suspected that he spent many hours every week at handball. Afterward, there would be massages and a steam room....

"Sorry to keep you waiting," Kirkpatrick said suavely, seating the man in a comfortable chair.

Wentworth remained standing and Auruckner glared at him, evidently desiring to be alone with the Commissioner. Wentworth blandly ignored the millionaire's hostility, lighted a cigarette. Finally the millionaire spoke after clearing his throat impressively:

"Hrrmph! Hate to do this, Commissioner," he said. "Truth is, I want a favor. Hrrmph! My daughter, this afternoon. If I can avoid publicity...."

Wentworth noticed with amazement that Auruckner's neck was turkey-red. The old duffer was embarrassed at asking a favor. He wasn't used to it. He gave orders and men snapped to attention, but he knew he couldn't approach Kirkpatrick that way. The Commissioner was a man of wealth in his own right. He had taken his present position first as a favor to the administration after a particularly filthy police scandal had broken out. He had remained since then by popular demand.

The public trusted Kirkpatrick and it would have been worth the mayor's job to dismiss him without a most excellent reason. Kirkpatrick was without political ambitions, though reform parties were constantly soliciting his candidacy. These factors colored Auruckner's manner. But it was plain that he resented the entire situation and was angry at being forced to come to police headquarters and petition a thing he felt he should receive as the inalienable right of wealth.

Kirkpatrick was curt. "We never involve innocent parties needlessly in publicity," he explained tartly, "Your daughter was not vitally involved this afternoon so far as I know, although I have not yet had an opportunity to question her." He shuffled some papers that had been placed on his desk in his absence. Wentworth saw the tightening of his lips that indicated a discovery. He waved a hand as if dismissing the question of Auruckner's daughter.

"What I really wanted you here for, Mr. Auruckner," he went on smoothly, "was to inquire how much you paid for having the Discus factory destroyed in Yonkers!"

For fully thirty seconds, Mark Auruckner stared at Kirkpatrick's keen, saturnine face. Then he snapped to his feet with a bull-bellow that could have been heard in the street outside. His chair kicked back from his knees, teetered and bumped to the floor.

"What do you mean by that?" he roared. "Hrrmph! I'll have an explanation of that, or I'll have your scalp, you… you…!" Words failed him utterly. The red of his neck deepened, took on a purplish tinge.

Wentworth picked up the chair and set it behind him. "Better sit down and take it easy, Mr. Auruckner," he said softly. "That high blood pressure of yours is apt to turn into apoplexy if you're not careful!"

KIRKPATRICK HAD not changed his position. He sat with his elbows on the desk, one hand resting on the reports. "Also," he went on quietly, "there is that matter of twelve murdered strikers in North Carolina. You might feel inclined to make some statement about that...."

"This is outrageous!" the millionaire screamed. "I won't submit to it! I was brought here under false pretenses...!" Kirkpatrick snapped abruptly to his feet, his fingers white, pressed on the desk-top.

"That will be enough hysterics," he said with a cold, incisive rasp. "You came here of your own free will. I object to your roaring. Sit down and control yourself or I'll have you put in a cell until you can talk intelligently."

Auruckner's mouth opened and closed spasmodically. The color deepened still more in his flabby cheeks. He lifted a hand to his throat, tore his collar, dropped panting into the chair. Wentworth seated him expertly, stepped before him.

"I gather, Kirk, that the reports confirmed my suspicions?" he asked quietly.

"They did," Kirkpatrick agreed savagely, "Auruckner is the owner of the Discus plant that was destroyed by lightning; he has a large interest in the textile mill where a lightning bolt killed a dozen strikers; he owns a big block of stock in the elevated railway company, and was especially active in the move to abolish the Mercer branch. Furthermore, Brandon Early is employed in his laboratories! Can you give me any good reason, Auruckner, why you shouldn't be charged with complicity in the murders of nearly a hundred persons by lightning?"

CHAPTER 7
VICTORY—AND DEFEAT

AGE IS a matter of spirit. A woman of seventy-six can be younger than a woman of fifty if the inner being keeps bright. And a husky, healthy man of fifty-five, a giant in the world of finance, can become ancient overnight—when the spirit is sucked out of him. Mark Auruckner was like that. He had been blustering and husky in his belligerent anger. Now, suddenly, he had become very old. The flesh of his cheeks was flabby; his throat drooped in folds. His eyes went bleary and his head sagged.

It had been a great many years since anyone had forced Mark Auruckner to act human. It sapped the strength out of him, but he did not completely lose his grip. "This is preposterous!" he said weakly. "You'll answer to me before courts for those wild statements."

"Do you want to confess now, or later?" Wentworth back snapped at him. "If you talk now and tell us how to get hold of the men who are using the lightning, it would be easier for you."

"I won't talk." The millionaire was regaining some of his strength. He jerked his bald, fuzz-covered head and some of his courage flowed back into him. "Am I under arrest?" he demanded hoarsely.

Kirkpatrick grinned at him, a thin, hard grin. "What would you think?"

"I want to see my lawyer!" Auruckner squalled suddenly. "I won't talk till I've seen my lawyer!"

Wentworth turned, winked at Kirkpatrick. "Mr. Auruckner is too distinguished a man to arrest like this, Kirk," he said. "Don't you think we should allow him to go home and break the news of his disgrace to his wife gently?"

Kirkpatrick scowled at Wentworth, glared into Auruckner's hopefully lifted face. "I don't see any reason for doing that," he growled. "A crook's a crook. Seventeen of my policemen have been murdered."

"Auruckner had no hand in that," Wentworth pleaded urgently. "Perhaps if we show him a little consideration, he will tell us how to find the men behind those killings."

Auruckner sat silent, but his eyes shifted anxiously from Wentworth to Kirkpatrick. Finally, the Commissioner shrugged his square shoulders. "You may go," he informed Auruckner, "but I warn you that any move to leave the city, and I'll clap you in a cell."

Auruckner nodded vehemently, eagerly. He stood in front of the desk and held out a trembling hand. "You're a gentleman, sir," he murmured. "I appreciate this."

Kirkpatrick stiffened behind his desk. His face was hard as rock. "Get out, you crook!"

Auruckner flinched from the words. He wavered toward the door. His paunch seemed suddenly too heavy for him to carry. It dragged his shoulders forward.

"Why did you urge that?" Kirkpatrick demanded angrily of Wentworth. "Auruckner's guilty as hell!"

Wentworth agreed with a nod and a small twisted smile on his mouth. "Yes, but there isn't a damn' thing against him, Kirk. You know that."

"Certainly not!" Kirkpatrick was still angry. "And when he gets to a lawyer, he'll find that out and we'll have gained nothing. We might have cracked him here."

"Not a chance!" Wentworth disagreed, shaking his head. "For a moment, there was a vague possibility that he might talk, but he got over that. We'll be able to find out more by tracing his movements and communications during the next few days, than...."

HE BROKE off as a staccato, stammer-fag roar of shots broke out in the street. Wentworth sprang to the window in time to see Auruckner's heavy figure slammed against the police station steps by a blast of gunfire—to see him crumple in a motionless huddle on the concrete. It was all pitifully clear in the glare of the street light. A coupé was leaping forward full throttled; a man was just drawing in the muzzle of a machine gun.

Wentworth's hand flashed to his shoulder holster, was out like a flicker of light. He fired through the glass office window, pumping three shots into the dark interior of the coupé. The ear-splitting crash of the gun in that confined space mingled with the icy tinkle of the broken plate-glass pane. Wentworth slammed three more slugs at the front wheels of the ear, watched it wobble, plunge toward the left curb. He held his seventh shot, waiting.

With a bounce, the coupé cleared the curb and rammed head-on against the wall of a building across the narrow street. It recoiled, and a man slammed out of the left door, darted around its rear with the machine gun cuddled against his hip. The muzzle was flickering with bullet flame, and the man crazily swept the windows of the police station with chattering gun-fire.

Wentworth deliberately fired his seventh shot. The machine gunner's head snapped back as if his neck had been broken by a hammer blow. His hands clawed his head frenziedly; then he pitched forward over the machine gun. Wentworth hurled his automatic savagely to the floor. Alarm bells were clanging in the halls. The carrot-topped police guard slammed into the room with a service revolver drawn in his hand.

"It's all right, Cassidy!" Kirkpatrick's sharp voice rang out. The policeman bolstered his revolver, snapped a salute and went out. Policemen were pouring into the street now, grouping around the bodies of the gunman and the millionaire.

Wentworth whirled toward the door. "Auruckner may still be alive!" Kirkpatrick was not two paces behind as they raced through the hall and down the stairs. The broad steps that led to the street seemed endless, but finally Wentworth was kneeling beside the riddled body of the millionaire. He lifted the old head with its crown of fuzzy, silvery hair.

Auruckner's eyes were open, but already glazing in a death spasm. "You're dying!" Wentworth snapped at the elderly man. "You can't die without doing your best to clear the records! Who did you hire to use the lightning?"

The bloodless, withered lips moved. Wentworth bowed close. "… wrong!" the whisper came. "Early was…."

A gurgling rattle of breath and the man collapsed. Life was gone. Wentworth lowered the fuzzy old head gently to the cold concrete and rose heavily.

What the devil did Auruckner mean? Were they wrong about Early, or had Auruckner been wrong? Was Early the guilty man?

"Damn it, this death is going to complicate things for us, Kirk," Wentworth said savagely. "Every man who has hired those lightning killers will read the truth behind this. They will know, that if the gangsters dared to kill a millionaire on the steps of the police station, their own lives are not safe anywhere. They won't talk!"

A policeman with a gold badge, a sergeant, strode up to Kirkpatrick. "That was beautiful shooting, sir," he said. "Three bullets through the window of the car smashed the hood's hip and pelvis. He's dead now. The other man was hit dead-center in the forehead."

WENTWORTH LAUGHED sharply, turned and strode back into the police station. Sure, he could shoot. Why not? He had spent a life-time of practice, until shooting and aim were as instinctive to him as pointing a finger. But where was his vaunted cleverness? He should have realized that Auruckner's life was in danger, that any one as clever as this fantastic Man from Mars would have been prepared for a thing of this sort. Aronk Dong would have realized that some one of those who hired the lightning would confess. And he would have been looking for a chance to teach them a lesson in discretion. Auruckner's visit to headquarters had been ideal for his purpose.

No, none of the men they might now draw into the police net would talk. He had discovered the motives behind the wholesale killings, but it had accomplished nothing.

Wentworth, inside Kirkpatrick's office, paced savagely back and forth. His right fist was clenched and his brows were scowling. Finally he took his brown *borsalina* from Kirkpatrick's wardrobe, jerked it on and hurried out of the building. He forgot his automatic, lying where he had hurled it on the floor. He forgot his stick, with its secret, slim blade of steel. Kirkpatrick called out to him as he clattered down the back stairs, but Wentworth only waved a hand in abrupt farewell.

He reached the sidewalk and stood, flat-footed, staring about him. The wind was chill after the rain. Broken clouds let through the faint rays of a dying moon. He rammed his good fist savagely into his coat pocket whirled on his heel and strode along the street His head was down and he was plunged in dark thoughts. An automobile hummed up beside him. "Taxi, mister?"

Wentworth shook his head and pounded on. Footsteps on the sidewalk behind jerked him up short. He whirled, stared at the taxi driver, who had alighted from his cab. The man was holding a short-barreled, heavy revolver with its muzzle aimed at Wentworth.

"Taxi, mister?" he said again. There was an impudent grin on his face.

Wentworth stood on braced feet and his eyes were hard and angry. In his self-wrath, Wentworth had permitted an enemy to catch him unaware. But evidently the man had no immediate intention of killing him, else he could have been shot down as he walked.

With a sudden, reckless laugh, Wentworth stepped toward the cab. "Yes, I do want a taxi!" he said. "Take me to Aronk Dong, the Lion Man of Mars!"

He stepped into the darkness of the cab, and he was smiling. He realized that he was without arms, but at the moment nothing seemed important except that he might face the Lion Man again. He laughed brittlely when a revolver prodded into his ribs inside the cab, and a masked man made room for him on the rear seat.

"That was exactly what I wished of *you*," the man murmured, with a trace of a French accent, "To take *me* to the Lion Man!"

Wentworth twisted in his seat to stare at the man: "I haven't the least idea where to find him!"

There was a snarl from behind the mask. Cold menace was in the man's reply: "Perhaps we can find a way to refresh your memory!" he snapped.

CHAPTER 8
MADMAN'S CONQUEST

AT THE instant Wentworth, unarmed and harassed, was seized by the masked man with the French accent, the Lion Man was in New Jersey, lounging comfortably in the tonneau of a rich limousine. He stroked his heavy mustaches with the knuckles of his right hand, and his half-closed eyes were well pleased.

"But why?" the girl beside him insisted, "do you bring me out here? I thought all your attacks were to be made in New York tonight."

The Lion Man chuckled and continued to fondle his mustaches. His heavy mane was uncovered, and smoothly combed, it made his head seem far larger than normal. He made no answer. Above the speeding car, the night was a black smother of gathering clouds. The earlier storm had failed to clear the atmosphere; another was fast gathering. The glimmer of the lightning was distant, but almost continuous.

Past them, on the road, automobiles roared at top speed, rocketing at seventy and eighty miles an hour. The hiss and thunder of the engines, sweeping by, made a harsh rhythm against the background of rumbling thunder. The faces of the drivers, faintly seen in the reflected glow of dash-lights, were strained and white. At a filling station, the operator was hurriedly locking his door. A moment later, he took to his heels, floundered out into the level meadows that stretched on either side of the four-laned roadway.

Aronk Dong found the entire scene vastly amusing. His chuckling was unceasing, like the purring of a great contented cat. The girl tried another query, then sank back on the cushions with her dark, questioning eyes covertly on the Lion Man. Dark hair curled out from under a pert hat. She was Bets Decker. Her hand went out hesitantly to his arm.

"I still don't see why you had me tortured like that," she said slowly. "It was cruel, cruel!"

"I had to be sure," the man muttered. "Alice Auruckner turned on me the first moment suspicion pointed my way. But you—!" He threw a great arm about her shoulders, drew her over against him, "You are loyal despite everything! You don't approve, but you trust me!"

"Yes," Bets Decker whispered against his shoulder. "I trust you. Bu…."

"Don't call me that!" Dong's voice was a snarl.

"I don't see why it matters," Bets lifted her eyes to his whiskered face. "I don't see why you have to hide your face from me when we're alone, either."

"I've told you," the Lion Man grated harshly, "that it's very dangerous. You mustn't even think of me by the name you started to pronounce. You might blurt it out in public sometime."

Bets sighed deeply. There was an odd light deep in her black eyes. Much of the color had drained from her face and it was wan and hopeless. "Dearest," she complained, "there are so many things I don't understand. Do you really have to destroy buildings and kill people? Surely, the world will believe in your greatness without such crimes."

Aronk Dong pushed her away roughly. "There can be no belief except through fear," he snarled. "The world has rejected me as a faker. Only you and these rats who do my bidding will believe…."

HE LEANED forward abruptly, staring up at the gathering storm clouds and rapped sharply on the glass that separated him from the chauffeur. The man swerved obediently to the side of the road. They were on the crest of a hill. A half-mile away, glittering now and again in the dance of the lightning, showed a great field of oil-filled storage-tanks. There were illuminated signs on those nearest the road. They read:

Special Hi-Test Gas
of the
Jonoco Company

Bets Decker seized his arm with both hands, her face twisted and white. "No, dear, not that!" she cried. "Surely, not that!"

Aronk Dong thrust her violently into the corner, but she pushed herself up on valiant arms and swayed toward him. "Please, dear," she pleaded. "Really, this isn't necessary. People believe in you now. They must! See how all the autos speed fast as people try to escape your lightnings! Look how frightened all their faces are!"

"Shut up!" Aronk Dong snarled. He was leaning forward tensely, staring with wide eyes at the illuminated field. His nostrils dilated and thinned. A sharp exclamation of joy snarled from his lips. One of the largest tanks began to show little dancing, blue sparks of electric flame. The fires flickered and jumped like weird candle-flame, leaping into thin air and darkness, reappearing an instant later. Off on the outskirts of the tank field, a siren moaned into life, its throaty whine rising and falling eerily on the storm-tossed air. Winds were sweeping roughly across the road, sucking up whirls of dust and paper trash, whirling it in mad-dervish spirals before the diffused lights of the limousine's headlights.

"Now!" Aronk Dong whispered.

In an office at the outskirts of the tank field, an excited young man in khaki breeches and shirt, with a red company insignia scrawled on his pocket, jammed the siren open and darted for the door. Overhead, the wail of the fire-signal was soughing a note of despair. A girl with a red sweater drawn on over her gingham dress ran behind him.

"Don't leave me, Sam!" she cried. She stumbled and shouted after the man in khaki. He wheeled a red motorcycle, equipped with hand fire-extinguishers, out of a small, red shed and pumped on the kick-crank. The girl sobbed up to him and hiked up her gingham skirt to straddle the rear mudguard.

The motor started with a staccato roar and the boy turned to her, shouting, gesturing toward the office.

"You can't do that in your condition," he shouted at her sharply.

He tried to loosen her hold upon the saddle of the motorcycle, but she clung stubbornly, weeping.

"If you're going to die, I'm going with you," she sobbed. "All three of us will die together. That lightning! I came over to be with you. Please, Sam!" She lifted her face. Her nose was swollen with crying; her eyes were red. The boy stared at her, frowning. Suddenly he cupped her tear-wet face in his hands and pressed his lips to hers. Without another word, he sprang to the saddle of the motorcycle and sent it cavorting in among the steel tanks with their protective ditches and bunkers. He was racing toward the tank that sparked with dancing, blue flames.

Up on the hill, a half mile away, the Lion Man repeated, "Now! Now!"

THE LIGHTNING was marching up like mobile artillery. The cannonade was continuous. The livid fire glimmered on a globular, floating shape drifting downwind as stealthily as a hunting wolf. Aronk Dong threw back his head and laughed. A blinding, blue-white glare lighted up his face, smeared it with black shadows through which his eyes burned. Bets Decker screamed wildly, an echo of the unheard cry of that girl in gingham down by the sparking tank, as she, too, glimpsed the drifting balloon and flung up a pointing finger.

Sam stared upward, then dropped the extinguisher and gathered her in his arms. His head was flung back and the wind smothered a defiant shout on his lips. He shook a fist at the slinking, gray shape directly overhead. For an instant, those two heroic figures were outlined in blue-white fire. It skipped and played over them in a demon dance, then there was an overwhelming lightning flash.

The steel tank split like a melon. A deluge of gasoline swept outward and the blue, dancing fires became a leaping, orange holocaust. The entire tidal wave of gasoline blew up in a devastating gust of living flame. Liquid fire was strewn a quarter mile over the landscape. Sam and his wife? Nothing....

In the limousine on the hill, Aronk Dong laughed long and heartily. The windows of his car shivered and rattled to the beat of the concussion. A gust of explosive wind made the car tremble, but he felt no more than that. The glory of his destruction claimed him.

Finally, the Lion Man leaned forward and tapped the glass again. The limousine turned in a wide, slow circle and loafed back toward the city through the gusting of the wind and the drum-beat of the slashing rain. The windshield wipers sloshed sturdily, smearing away the water. Bets Decker shivered uncontrollably. Shudder after shudder shook her body. She was moaning softly.

The Lion Man's mirth peeled on, rivaling the thunder. He was drunk with laughter. "Thus will I crush the entire country, the entire world!" he screamed, shaking both great fists into the air. "I'll kill and destroy until they all crawl to me on their knees...."

Bets Decker's small fearful hand went out to his arm. "Please, dear," she whispered. "Talk to me, I'm frightened."

Aronk Dong twisted toward her, staring with widened eyes that were full of the madness of conquest. He reached out his massive arms and crushed her to him; ground her lips beneath his... He threw back his head and bellowed: "You and all the world!" he swore. "I'll have the world!"

CHAPTER 9
THE PRECIOUS PAWN

BUT WENTWORTH could not know of all this horror. He leaned back against the cushions and shrugged at the menace in the masked man's voice.

"Would you mind very much," he asked, with a bored sigh,

"not pressing quite so hard with that revolver? I have felt more comfortable muzzles."

"It would save you much unpleasantness, *m'sieur,*" the armed man hissed, "if you would talk here and now."

Wentworth wrinkled his nose delicately at a whiff of over-ripe fish from the river-bank. They were on South street, headed for the Battery.

"I never," he admitted, "cared for unpleasantness of any kind."

"Then talk!"

"Certainly," said Wentworth amicably. "I was a fool to walk out of police headquarters without a gun. I am even more fool-ish to permit a strange automobile to stop beside me before I am aware of it. And what is more…."

The man snarled and the revolver muzzle rasped against a rib. Wentworth complained mildly, but his jocular speech was far from mirroring his true frame of mind. He was furious at the ease with which he had allowed himself to be captured. He was puzzled about the man who held him prisoner, and bewildered by the possible motives behind the man's activities. A masked man obviously could not be the law. Nor was this a new Avenger, who sought, as did the Spider, to eliminate a menace to human-ity. What then, exactly, was his purpose? Wentworth doubted that direct questioning would accomplish anything. He sought to extract information from him through irritation.

The taxi reached the Battery and circled, heading northward again along the Hudson River waterfront.

"You are taking a very indirect method to reach the Lion Man's headquarters," Wentworth drawled indifferently.

"I think that I shall *garrote* you," the man behind the mask grated. "Yes, I am quite sure that I shall *garrote* you, slowly… You are much too witty to die fast."

Wentworth nodded his head. Yes, it all checked; accent, the occasional *"m'sieur"* and now *garrote,* weapon of the *apache* of Paris. There was little doubt that he was in the hands of some French criminal. But why would a Frenchman be horning in on the battle between the Spider and the Lion Man?

"Come," he said, "we should not be enemies. Both of us want to exterminate the Lion Man. Let's join forces."

A harsh chuckle bubbled from the masked man. "You were a bit slow in arriving at that conclusion, *m'sieur.*"

Wentworth shrugged. "Does that matter? Better late than never, *n'est pas, m'sieur?*"

"Ah, yes!" his captor agreed. "You are ready then, to lead me to this so-named Lion Man? So far as I can learn, M'sieur Wentworth, you are the only man who has yet met this animal. The papers tell me of that. They report to me also that you are an amateur criminologist of such great fame that in the pas' you have often mistake' yourself for the Spider. *Allors, m'sieur,* I cannot doub' you have foun' a way to fin' this Lion Man!"

Wentworth laughed shortly. "If I knew where that creature was, I wouldn't have been walking along the street slowly. I would have been flying, bringing death in each hand!"

THE FRENCHMAN questioned Wentworth sharply for several minutes. Finally he seemed convinced that the American did not know where to find Aronk Dong. He sat silent then while the cab pushed on northward, idling now beneath the elevated motor-highway that runs from Canal Street to Riverside Drive. Lightning was performing a wild death-dance in the south, over New Jersey. There was a ruddy glow against the black clouds that drew Wentworth's brows down in a hard knot over his eyes. "That will be more of the Lion Man's work!" he muttered.

Though Wentworth did not know it, the glow was from the blazing storage tank fields. Even at this moment, Aronk Dong, drunk with mad laughter, was shouting his dream of conquest into the beat and roar of the elements. Wentworth clenched his fists on his knees, anger flaming within him. He twisted abruptly toward the masked man and a gleam from a passing street light winked on the ready muzzle of the man's revolver.

"I don't know who you are," Wentworth began, "but if you are intent on ridding the world of Aronk Dong...."

"But, *m'sieur,*" the masked man protested, "I said nothing of the sort. I say only that I am interes' in *findin'* this one. In fac', I want so little to kill him that I mus' ask you promise to spare him should you two meet!"

"I promise you this:" Wentworth replied. "When I find him, I'll be careful not to let him die too quickly or too easily!"

The Frenchman breathed, "So!" He sat quiet for a considerable while. Then he raised his voice in a command to the chauffeur: *"Chez moi*—to my place!" The taxi picked up speed, whirling corners on whining rubber. It spun finally into an alley. When it stopped, close walls made the beat of the engine resound loudly. Doors grated shut behind the car and the engine died. Lights blazed overhead and four men stood at each door with leveled guns.

Wentworth smiled grimly, as he surveyed the faces of the men. All of them were small. He had never seen a more villainous group, even in the worst dives of the Montmartre. But the type was the same—these were the rats of Paris, *les Apaches!*

A flash of understanding came to Wentworth. He had made it his business to know the underworlds of all countries. He knew the Bertillon measurements, the *portrait parlait,* of a hundred of the high society of crookdom. He flashed a glance at the left hand of the little man and his guess was confirmed. The little finger was doubled in against the palm, the relic of an old knife fight.

"You are Toussaints Louvaine!" Wentworth exclaimed. "You steal the secrets of nations—sell them to the highest bidder. You want to get the secret of man-made lightnings from Aronk Dong and peddle it. By heaven, you would precipitate the world into war if you peddled that weapon to the wrong nation!"

Toussaints Louvaine shrugged. He reached up and uncovered a shrewd, pointed face; he brushed upturned mustaches with his finger tips to see that the mask had not disturbed them. "I am mos' grateful you have recognize me," the Frenchman said. "The mask was very uncomfortable."

WENTWORTH CURSED. "You can be calm!" he rasped. "You never fight in time of war. You would get rich and fat while men are slaughtered! By God. I believe you hope the secret of the lightnings in the hands of a greedy power will promote a war!"

Toussaints Louvaine looked at Wentworth with small, bright

eyes, still brushing his mustaches delicately with his finger-tips. "There will alway' be war, my frien'," he said lightly. "You can no more blame me than you can blame soldiers for drillin' and learnin' to use the bayonet. And I am not all bad! I offer the secrets firs' to *la belle* France. If she cannot afford it..." He shrugged. A smile flashed over his face, sharpened it with a gleam of narrow, long teeth. "In this case, I suspec' it would take a very rich nation to affor' the secret. Therefore, I mus' reques' again that when you meet the Lion Man he shall not be harm'!"

"I'll be damned if I'll promise that," Wentworth snarled and each word was squeezed out between his teeth with an effort.

Louvaine lifted both palms at his sides, motioned to the *Apaches*. Wentworth was seized immediately by the four men and bound securely. A filthy gag was thrust into his mouth and light, powerful lines bit into his wrists and ankles. He was tossed against the wall in the glare of the taxi headlights. He heard a man climb into the seat, clap the door shut.

"Allors, m'sieur," Toussaints Louvaine laughed. "I trus' you res' mos' pleasantly. Should you stir unduly, Francois will run the taxi over you!..."

It was an hour later—an hour during which Wentworth had fought vainly against his bonds—that he was jerked to his feet and half-dragged, half-carried through a dark passageway and up steps into a smelly hall—thence into a broad, well-lighted room that was furnished in the stuffy, bad taste of the nineties.

Toussaints Louvaine laughed at his wrathful eyes and unfastened the gag with deft fingers. "You will need your tongue," he said. "We have taken a hostage to guarantee the life of Aronk Dong." He signed to his men.

They opened a door across the room, brought a woman, bound hand and foot. They thrust her into a heavy overstuffed chair. Wentworth's heart hammered in his throat; rage choked him as he recognized the proud high carriage of her head!

The woman was Nita van Sloan!

CHAPTER 10
A THIN TRAIL

A SMILE at once mocking and deprecatory flickered across the Frenchman's thin, mustached lips as he met Wentworth's furious glare.

"I greatly regret that you make this necessar'," he told Wentworth gently. "But you would not consen' to capturin' the Lion Man alive. So…" He shrugged. "I t'ink now you will not refuse my little reques.'"

Nita's warm violet eyes met Wentworth's with brave uncon-cern. There was a small, unwavering smile on her lips. Long ago, when their love had triumphed over all their efforts against it, she and Wentworth had made a bargain together. They would fight the Spider's battles side by side; but if ever it became neces-sary to choose between the life of one of them and the good of the people, that life should be sacrificed unhesitatingly.

Nita was remembering that now, Wentworth realized, and she was ready for the sacrifice. Her smile told him that. Before this, criminals had kidnapped Nita and held her hostage to cripple the Spider. Wentworth, in every such case, had answered threat with threat. Harm Nita, and each man involved would die terribly, marked with the seal of the Spider. He had forced himself to disregard that Nita was in danger.

"Come," Toussaints Louvaine urged, "it is one little t'ing that I as' of you. Jus' that you let the Lion Man live until I can purchase his weapon. Once that is done, *pouf!* I do not care what you do wit' him. In fac' it woul' suit me ver' well if he were to die—afterward. *Hein?*"

Wentworth glared at him with a cold venom that caused the man's hand to creep toward his gun. "I know that you hate me, *M'sieu,*" Louvaine said, "but *pouf!*" he snapped his fingers. "You are nothin' beside Toussaints Louvaine!" He walked up to Nita and tapped her shoulder. "She is my guarantee of safety, *hein?* Take her away!" He gestured to his men and Nita was pulled backward toward the door.

"Forget about me, Dick!" she called. "Do what is best."

Wentworth fought for calmness. But fierce anger rose in him. He forced words harshly from his tight throat.

"Louvaine, if any harm is done her, I promise that you shall die—yet live to wish for death many times!"

Louvaine fought to meet the Spider's direct, burning gaze twice before he succeeded. The color fled from his face, left it paper-white.

"You threaten, eh, *M'sieur?*" he jeered. "You threaten, wit' your arms tie' behind your bac'? But enough of this! I've said she shall not be 'armed if you do as I wish. Fin' the Lion Man;

keep him alive until I can deal wit' him. That is all. Come now, your promise!"

Wentworth's angry glare died slowly. He hated Louvaine and all he stood for. Nita's capture stirred his rage anew, but the Spider's cool, calm brain dictated that he use this man in his fight against the Lion Man. Louvaine had money and men, and both hunted Aronk Dong.

"I have proved to my own satisfaction," Wentworth said slowly, making his voice expressionless with a powerful effort of will, "that the Lion Man hires out his lightning to whomever wishes to destroy something. We cannot trace him through those who have already hired him because he has terrorized them by murder. Our only chance is to present ourselves as wanting something destroyed."

"But that is *magnifique!*" Toussaints Louvaine exclaimed. " 'Ow will you arrange that?"

WENTWORTH SHRUGGED. "That is your task. I can tell you only what to do. While you try that method, I shall use others. Do you agree that once Aronk Dong is located, and you are put in touch with him, Miss van Sloan shall be released whether you or I make the contact?"

Louvaine nodded, his small eyes glistening. "It is agree'!" He gestured grandly. Wentworth was seized again and carried roughly to the taxi which had brought him. Twenty minutes later, he was shoved out on a dark, East Side street. A knife clanged to the pavement beside him. It took the Spider five minutes to free himself. He gripped the knife and stared with heavy-lidded eyes along the way the cab had traveled. Then hurried toward more peopled streets.

His first action was to call Kirkpatrick and warn him of this new complication in the battle. Of Nita, he said nothing.

"We have a new ally in the fight." Kirkpatrick informed him. "Cosmos Delane, of Auruckner's laboratories, has come to our aid. He is going to try to find a way to make homes and buildings immune to lightning. It is apparent by now that ordinary lightning rods are of no service, but it is barely possible that Delane will find some new safeguard."

Wentworth stared blankly at the instrument before him in the booth. "Did this Delane volunteer his services?" he queried.

"How did you guess?"

Wentworth smiled thinly at the mouthpiece. "My suspicious nature," he said shortly. "It's remarkable how often these expert advisors prove to be associated with the criminals."

"That's nonsense!" Kirkpatrick said.

"Of course," Wentworth conceded. "Now, Kirk, I want a favor of you. Send word to the fire-alarm headquarters in Central Park that they are to permit me to listen in on all calls, will you?"

"Sounds innocent enough," Kirkpatrick grunted. "I'll have Cassidy attend to it." The connection was broken and Wentworth hailed a taxi.

At the fire-alarm headquarters, two men are always on duty. One stands beside a long bank of filing cabinets; before him is a complicated machine, with big wheels and a paper scroll. The other man sits beside a telephone. When an alarm comes, the man at the files fingers through a case hurriedly and extracts a

Wentworth dared not thrust out from behind the steel pillar even for a snap shot at his assailants.

perforated card with the number of the alarm upon it. He drops that into his complicated machine. Instantly, a new series of numbers begins to tap out on the bell at one end of the room. This takes care of equipment shifts to cover the engine that was ordered out. This is the heart of the entire great fire-control system of New York City, which has been called the finest in the world. It was to this room, which has taken the place of the watch tower of olden times, that Wentworth made his way. He perched upon a tall stool, watching, the firemen with bright eyes. He sat silently smoking while the alarms tapped in. When phone calls reported the details for the record, he asked always one question:

"What was the cause of the fire?"

The causes were various, but none interested him. He pored over old newspapers which lay in a corner. He discovered a series of articles on "Men from Mars," by Horace Jones and recalled the writer's prophecy at the club dinner that he could make a mint of money from Wentworth's information. Wentworth frowned over the details. The man's memory was amazing. There was a certain lurid authenticity that was strangely convincing. Perhaps he had some other sources of information. He would get his chemist friend, Professor Brownlee, whose place was not so far from Jones' Connecticut home, to make some inquiries for him. Wentworth got Professor Brownlee on the phone.

IT WAS five o'clock in the morning. Wentworth's eyes were heavy with sleep when the answer to his question, "What was the cause?" concerning a tenement fire on the East Side, brought him to his feet with a jerk.

"Lightning," the fireman grunted, bending over a yard-wide report fastened to a slanting desk by thumbtacks.

Instantly, Wentworth crossed to the desk, peered over the man's shoulder. The fireman twisted his head about. One cheek was drawn and scarred by fire and there was a discontented droop to his mouth.

"Now what?" he rasped.

"Just tell me the owner," Wentworth said affably, "and where he lives, and I'll be on my way!"

The man grunted, jabbed a blunt finger at an entry on the lined paper before him. Wentworth read the words, strode jauntily toward the door. He was whistling softly as he shoved out of the old gray building in Central Park and sucked in a deep breath of the fresh morning air. The sky was brightening over behind the tall apartments of Fifth Avenue. The first rumbling of daily traffic had begun and all about him birds twittered.

He left the greenness of the park, signaled a taxi which sped him toward the upper West Side. He snapped a cigarette from the window with a nervous gesture and lit another. It was a very thin trail he followed, but no other had yet produced results. Brandon Early had vanished into the air like one of his own lightning balloons. Police had trailed Bets Decker in hope of locating Early, and she, too, had disappeared since she had interrupted their dinner at the club. Alice Auruckner—Wentworth's eyes narrowed thoughtfully—it was doubtful if anything would develop through her, especially since her father was dead.

Nita could not help him. Deliberately, he tried to drive all thought of her from his mind. But the thought of her brave, unwavering smile, the dear courage of her last words to him, rose tormentingly to plague him. The smoke from the cigarette seared his lungs. There was an inch-long, glowing, hot coal on the end of it. He flung it through the window.

Wentworth became aware that the taxi was swerving to the curb, that the driver was unlatching the door. The apartment where Louis Baum, the owner of the building which lightning had wrecked lived, stood on a corner of upper Broadway, north of 172nd Street. Wentworth phoned Ram Singh to rent a large sedan with curtained windows, and to drive to the place. After all, if he was planning to kidnap the Lion Man, he must be prepared. He smiled at the thought, pushed into a small, dirty restaurant labeled COFFEE POT in big sprawling letters. He drank many cups of black coffee.

This early in the day, it was possible to watch the main door of the apartment building from a distance. Later, he would have to move closer. And sooner or later, Wentworth was sure, a collection man from Aronk Dong would call on this man whose building had been destroyed by lightning. It was unlikely that full payment for the service had been made in advance. When the collection man came, Wentworth intended to trail him to Aronk Dong's headquarters. It was a very roundabout lead, but ultimately it should take him to the Lion Man himself.

SLIGHTLY OVER a half-hour later, Ram Singh wheeled past the COFFEE POT in a heavy, black sedan. Wentworth frowned, then laughed. The thing had a funereal aspect. When, presently, Ram Singh parked the car and straddled a stool near

Wentworth, Wentworth learned why. It had been rented from a funeral director.

Ram Singh had wisely unwound his turban from his head and wore a cap. He did not say much when the counter man was near, but ordered coffee and pretended to drink it. Actually, he would have touched none of the food in the place. His religion stipulated stringently how his victuals were to be prepared. His words came from motionless lips.

"Kirkpatrick, *sahib*, has been 'phoning for an hour. He had a report that *missie sahib* was kidnapped, and the *missie sahib* is not in her apartment."

Wentworth nodded with tightening lips. "I know." Presently he left the restaurant. Three minutes later, Ram Singh joined him, and Wentworth told him the object of their watch. The Hindu's eyes glittered with an eager light.

"Then, *sahib*, we may fight, thou and I? He lapsed into Hindustani and his white teeth glistened between curving lips. His hand strayed beneath his coat and Wentworth knew those powerful, slim fingers fingered the hilt of his nine-inch knife.

"Yes, my warrior," Wentworth agreed softly. "But remember, the Lion Man must be taken alive. That is why I needed a car equipped with curtains on all windows. The *missie sahib's* life depends upon his being taken alive."

"*Wah!*" Ram Singh snarled. "It is a thing not to my liking, *sahib*. But... I hear and obey."

Wentworth nodded, left Ram Singh on guard while he strolled about the apartment house, seeking a rear entrance. The collection man from Aronk Dong might wish to enter secretly...

At the corner, Wentworth halted, suddenly, covered his surprise by lifting his cigarette to his lips. His breath hissed out slowly. A coupé was backing into a half-alley that, he saw, would reach to the apartment house he watched. And as the coupé turned, he caught the light on its rear window. That window was of two panes, parted in a vertical slit in the middle—obviously a gun port in bullet-proof glass!

Wentworth completed lighting his cigarette and walked on carelessly. He passed within ten feet of the hood of the car, glanced at it incuriously and paced by. The instant he was out of sight, he quickened his pace and circled the block to where Ram Singh watched the front door.

"Our quarry are there," he said rapidly. "I'll drive the sedan. Get a taxi and follow me as far back as possible. These men may have an escort car."

He hurried to the sedan, donned a uniform cap that he had ordered Ram Singh to bring, and from the ever-present kit beneath his left arm, extracted hair which he rapidly fashioned into a small mustache. He slumped into the seat, round-shouldered and careless-handed, and maneuvered to a spot where he could watch both the alley's mouth and the building's front entrance. Within minutes, Ram Singh walked out of the front door, paused and wiped an eye with his handkerchief. Wentworth's heart pounded with excitement. His suspicions were correct; the men from the armored coupé had entered Louis Baum's apartment. He was certain now they were Aronk Dong's agents.

When the coupé rolled out of the alley and drifted up to a red traffic signal, Wentworth turned the corner and coasted after it, spurted past as the lights changed again. He did not make the mistake of remaining behind them, or suiting his pace to theirs. On occasion he was two blocks ahead; then he would deliberately allow himself to be boxed behind a car making a left hand turn and forced to wait for a break in traffic. The armored coupé would skin past then and it would take him blocks to pass again.

He kept the trail eastward across town, southward again into the business district where the coupé paused a moment to drop a man before the mighty Cloud Spire on East Forty-second Street. At Wentworth's signal, Ram Singh trailed the man, reported that he had entered the office of Fulton Haybred, a contractor. The armored coupé drifted by again, hesitated before the Cloud Spire and rolled on again. Had the Spider been spotted? He couldn't be sure, but there was a tingling along his spine that seemed to warn of danger.

The man who had entered the building returned and stood on the curb. As Wentworth caught a glimpse of the circling coupé in his rear vision mirror, he pulled out from the curb and rolled down to the next street intersection. His mind raced back to the significance of that visit to the contractor's office. He knew Fulton Haybred, of course. The man had built half the skyscrapers in the city during the last fifteen years, but lately a rival firm had developed. A young engineer named McCorson, with apparently ample financial backing, had been competing quite successfully.

The coupé rolled alongside, but the driver did not look over at him. The two men inside seemed absorbed in conversation.

Wentworth decided he had not been spotted and followed as the car pushed on eastward. His mind returned to the skyscraper contractor. He recalled that there had been some recent publicity about the two competing firms but he could not remember its exact nature. His attention was yanked back to the pursuit when the coupé suddenly whirled left into First Avenue and then, for no obvious reason, slewed sideways and virtually blocked the street by slapping against a pillar of the elevated railway.

Wentworth kicked his brakes, stuck out his head and bawled at them in the best chauffeur manner. But he knew the reason behind the faked accident. The gangsters had spotted him and were blocking the way to keep him from escaping—to kill him. Well, thought Wentworth, gravely, there was nothing to keep him from killing them! He flung a swift glance into the rear-vision mirror fastened to a spare tire at the running board. Another coupé, almost identical with the one ahead, carrying two men, was turning the corner behind him. The Spider was trapped....

CHAPTER 11
SEAL OF THE SPIDER

WITH MOMENTUM Wentworth might have smashed through that coupé ahead and escaped, but it was impossible after he had made a dead stop. Wentworth knew the car behind would roll alongside on his left. A blaze of guns, and the Spider would be eliminated from the picture. Ram Singh, trailing in the taxi, would be too late. Even while these ideas flashed through his mind, the coupé was whirling up on his left side, the bullet-proof window parting in the middle for the death shot....

Wentworth's month twisted in a hard grin. He snapped flat on the cushion to his right, flung open the door and kicked himself head first out into the street. He clung to the door-handle and caught himself up in a half-crouch. The coupé was alongside now, but the bulk of the sedan was between him and the hungry gun that yawned from the window. He flung a swift glance up and down the street. A half-block behind him, a heavy truck was maneuvering slowly between the elevated pillars, blocking traffic. Yes, the trap had been cleverly planned. Flight to the sidewalk would expose him instantly to gunfire.

From a crouch beside the sedan, Wentworth flung himself to a steel pillar of the elevated railway. Behind him, a gun blasted and lead clanged against the steel, ricocheted and smacked a hole in a plate-glass store-window. Wentworth's automatic flashed to his hand and he pumped a bullet accurately through the gun-port slit in the window of the coupé. Only the man's shoulder was exposed, but he drilled that neatly. The man slumped sideways, clutching at his shoulder, and Wentworth fired again. The man's head was at the slit now, and the second bullet thudded through his skull. The driver of the second coupé whirled his machine to the left. It darted across First Avenue, jounced over the curb and slammed halfway into a shoemaker's shop, scattering glittering shreds of plate glass for twenty feet.

Even before it had reached the curb, the coupé's two doors were flung back like wings. From behind their cover, two men poured a drumming fire of bullets at Wentworth's narrow shield. Lead clanged against the steel pillar, raising a loud din. Windows behind him were soon in fragments. The scream and whine of bullets were echoed by shrieks as people on the sidewalks fled pell-mell. Automobile horns blared and scolded at the truck blockade, but the hammer of guns stilled them. Their drivers swerved into side streets.

Wentworth dared not thrust out from behind his steel pillar even for a snap shot at his assailants. The girder against which he leaned was almost perfect for its purpose. It was a wide beam, shaped in crossed-section like a letter "I," with the hollowed-out portion turned toward Wentworth and toward his enemies. Wentworth turned sideways so that his shoulders were in the hollow, stepped upon the concrete base of the pillar, and toeing rivet heads, fought his way slowly upward.

It was slow, strenuous work. He was compelled to turn his wounded shoulder inward, rasping it against the metal, so as to leave his gun-hand free in case of surprise. The steel brought a dull agony. Sweat popped out on his forehead in beads, but he fought on. The beat of bullets against the steel was unceasing, and Wentworth suspected it covered the advance of a gunman.

He twisted his head to watch alertly for the first sign of new attack. Suddenly, he saw! A hand was thrust around the steel pillar, a hand with a gun. It blasted directly into the hollow where, a few minutes before, Wentworth had stood. Now the lead scorched under his shoe soles. Wentworth's lips pressed hard and thin against his teeth. He fired straight down into the arm, aiming as near the body as possible.

The gunman's arm jerked downward under the six-hundred-foot-pound assault of Wentworth's forty-five bullet, fired at almost point-blank range. It pulled the gunman off balance even as a scream of pain broke from his throat. The man stumbled and Wentworth's gun blasted again, blew in the top of his head.

The gunfire stopped with a sudden stillness that hurt the ears. In the abrupt quiet, a man screeched and stopped screeching with a strangling gurgle. Wentworth sprang to the ground. He had heard men cry out like that before this—when Ram Singh's knife pierced their throats. He stepped from behind the pillar and flinched aside as a gun blasted from the coupé which had caromed into the shop window. He slammed lead back, striving to find a vital target.

MINUTES SEEMED to have dragged past since the trap had been sprung, yet Wentworth knew from the fact that Ram Singh's taxi was just at the corner, and Ram Singh was just running forward with a second knife in his hand, that no more than seconds had elapsed since the coupé had whirled to block the Spider's path. Soon, though, police sirens would moan, and before that time the Spider must be gone. He snapped another shot into the back of the coupé, shouted a shrill warning to Ram Singh in Hindustani.

Beside the car that had blocked his path, a man lay flat on his face. From the back of his neck protruded the hilt of the knife that the Hindu had thrown. Suddenly, from the wrecked car, a man flung himself to the sidewalk. He rolled, sprang to his feet and doubled over, ran in a dodging zigzag up the street. Ram Singh's knife arm flashed back. His body rocked on his toes for the throw, but Wentworth stopped him with a shouted order.

"Let him live! We have killed enough to put fear of the Spider into their souls. One must be alive to lead us to the den of these rats."

Ram Singh checked his throw. Wentworth dropped instantly to his knees beside the man he had slain. He jerked him over on his back and, lips drawn back from his teeth, in a macabre grin, he pressed the base of his cigarette lighter to the corpse's forehead. When he lifted it, a vermilion, sprawling spider had been printed on the chilling flesh—*the seal of the Spider!* Now, at last, the Spider was alive again. Now, newspapers would shrill the news to the criminal world that the avenger of the innocent had risen from the dead to strike again at the foes of humanity.

Ram Singh was straightening above the second criminal as Wentworth got to his feet. The Hindu had wrenched his knife free. He wiped the glistening blade clean on the man's coat and whirled to pursue the single gangster who had been allowed to escape.

Without warning, without even a whisper of its siren, a police-car skated into the street. A policeman sprang out with a riot gun clutched in his hands. Wentworth barked a warning in Hindustani even as he flung himself flat behind the man he had slain. The riot gun blasted. He heard the slugs plunk soddenly into the corpse beside him, and he screamed, thrashing his arms and legs about. The cop plunged forward, pumping a new shell into the chamber of his weapon.

Wentworth knew that he had only a scant moment while the cop manipulated the mechanism. He twisted his automatic deliberately and slammed a bullet into the lock of the shotgun. The policeman reeled under the sledge-hammer blow of lead and the Spider was instantly on his feet. In three long leaps, he reached his sedan, crashed into reverse gear and darted backward. The first policeman was wringing his bullet-numbed hands, the smashed riot gun on the ground at his feet. He was unhurt, but for the moment, helpless. The second policeman was caught half-in, half-out of his Ford roadster and, though he gripped his revolver, he was in no position to fire.

Wentworth spun backwards around a corner to the left. He heard police lead clang, saw a silvery streak across the top of the hood where the bullet had glanced. Then a brick wall, the corner of a building, was between him and the vicious gun.

Seconds later, Wentworth spun north. His eyebrows were drawn down in a savage scowl. Ram Singh had left only a fraction of a second before that police car had whirled the corner, its siren silent. Chances were that at least two other police cars were converging on this same spot. If they had come by other streets, the faithful Hindu might be trapped between their converging lines.

Wentworth wrenched at the wheel again, sent the heavy sedan eastward, back toward the scene of the battle—toward the spot where the Spider seal told of his resurrection and where police cars were swarming…!

CHAPTER 12
A LEAD AT LAST

WENTWORTH HAD not gone a half-block toward First Avenue when he realized the full daring of the thing he was attempting. He had guessed right about the number of police who would rush to the scene. A detective cruiser—a sedan carrying four plainclothes men armed with everything from tear-gas bombs and revolvers to high-powered rifles and grenades—had halted at the corner. Its four men were deployed behind parked cars, guns blazing.

On the other side of First Avenue, a police roadster had halted and its two officers were firing, too. Wentworth slowed, then pushed on toward the battle. Were these men firing on Ram Singh? Gripping fear crowded his throat. Ringed about by six men against whom he, no more than the Spider, would fight, what chance would the brave Hindu have? Even as Wentworth coasted up toward the detectives, a triumphant shout went up from them and they dashed forward.

Wentworth started out into the tangle of First Avenue. Behind a steel pillar, a man had crumpled. Joy swelled Wentworth's heart. It was not Ram Singh, but the gangster the Hindu had pursued! Apparently, he had been trapped by the police and had preferred to shoot it out rather than be captured. Where, then, was Ram Singh?

Wentworth glanced about the avenue, along the side street. He glimpsed an arm waving from behind a car, and instantly, he sent the sedan lurching forward again. A detective spun toward him, flinging up a hand and shouting an order to halt. Wentworth started to obey. This man could have nothing against him, probably wanted only that he circle the block instead of crossing First Avenue before the shambles was cleared. But fifty feet behind the detective he glimpsed another policeman in uniform, pounding toward them, his face furiously red. It was the officer from whose hands Wentworth had shot the riot gun.

"Look out!" the officer shouted hoarsely. "The Spider's come to life! *That man is the Spider!*"

And the Spider was already in full flight. He braked to a quivering near-halt where he had caught the signal of a high-thrown arm, and Ram Singh sprang to the running board. Instantly Wentworth was under way again and the Hindu climbed inside, while the car moaned with mounting speed.

The detective cruiser had got under way with two of its crew behind the bulletproof windshield. With whooping siren, it was charging after Wentworth. Ram Singh twisted about in his seat, stared toward the pursuit.

"Two other cars, *sahib,*" he murmured, "besides that of the detectives, are behind us!"

Wentworth's lips pressed hard together. He swung his weight on the wheel, sent the car racing around the corner, took another turn to the left a moment later… and found the police still on his trail. He knew that one of those radio patrol cars would stop soon and an officer would hurl himself into a telephone booth. Then radio headquarters would know about the chase.

WENTWORTH DROVE almost automatically, doubling corners, smashing his way through frightened traffic that was split by the moaning sirens in his wake. A taxi-driver pushed his cab squarely into the center of the street, hopped out and ran. A tight grin tugged at Wentworth's lips. It wasn't the taxi driver's cab of course; it belonged to the company. He didn't mind risking some one else's property for the sake of the publicity he would get if the trick succeeded. The street was narrow and parked cars crowded close.

"Duck down!" Wentworth yelled at Ram Singh. "We're going to crash!"

He jerked the sedan as far to the right as possible, took the taxi on its right, front wheel and smashed it aside. The taxi pivoted, turned completely about. Wentworth was past, and the street was blocked again. Wentworth laughed sharply, bore down even harder on the accelerator and blasted across traffic against a light with his horn blaring. He raced straight ahead for three blocks, swung right. He was just slowing when a radio patrol-car whirled a corner not seventy-five feet ahead.

It jerked to a halt and the two cops flung out with guns in hand. A fender of the sedan had been crumpled by the crack-up. It ground now against the tire so that the scent of burnt rubber was thick. His car was identified all right. Those two police with their ready guns... Wentworth slapped on brakes, lifting both hands off the wheel, elevating them.

"Throw the car into second gear," he told Ram Singh swiftly.

The two police came forward warily behind thrust-out guns, one to either side. Ram Singh slid the gear shift forward and lifted his hands also.

"You've got me!" Wentworth snarled sullenly. "These damned radio cars!"

The two police were on each side now. Wentworth kicked the accelerator and the car lurched. "Duck!" he barked.

Ram Singh hunched down below the back of the cushion and the car rocketed straight forward toward crowded traffic. Risking a glance ahead, Wentworth managed a left turn that scraped fenders with a taxi.

"Get that cab and beat it north," Wentworth ordered.

Ram Singh flung open his door, leaped to the running board of the taxi. Wentworth saw the Hindu's nine-inch knife blade glint, saw the taxi-driver's livid face, and the cab skittered around a corner to the right. He swung to the left and, staring into the rear-vision mirror, saw that he had led the chase in his direction, that Ram Singh apparently was getting clear. He settled down to hard driving. The fender whined against the tire. It was only a question of time, he knew, before the hard steel wore through the casing and caused a blowout.

Glancing ahead, Wentworth saw that Park Avenue was the next street he would cross, saw that traffic was filing past in a slow, uninterrupted stream.

Two flower-laden phaetons with tops down loafed past, part of a funeral procession. Behind that came the hearse and a succession of cars filled with mourners. A sudden idea brought a thin, dubious grin to Wentworth's lips. If his car were not so battered... He flung a swift look behind. The police were having trouble moving the truck with which they had attempted to stop him. He glanced at the damages to his car. The left fender was crumpled, but the fender had worn the tire so that now it whined only occasionally. Undoubtedly there were bullet-holes in the car's back, but so far all the glass had escaped.

WENTWORTH SPUN around the corner into Park Avenue, paralleling the funeral. He reached behind him, snapped down the curtains so that all windows were covered. The end of the funeral was dragging past now. He wheeled his big sedan in at the extreme end, sticking close to the rear of the car ahead. The driver would not see him. All the shades of the rear were pulled down, including that on the back window, to shield the mourners from the gaze of the morbid curious, even as Wentworth's own shades were drawn down. He was so close to the other car that the fender, against the iron fence which divided Park Avenue's two lanes of traffic, would not easily be seen. And Wentworth, with the bored expression of a mortician's chauffeur, pulled his uniform cap snugly into place and drifted along at ten miles an hour.

With a whoop of sirens, two radio cars whirled out of a side-street and screeched along beside the funeral. Wentworth turned and stared at them curiously. One paused two blocks ahead beside a traffic policeman, then whirled on again. The funeral procession crawled on, swung eastward, past a cordon of police standing with drawn guns. They gave the funeral cortège no more than a glance, though one stared curiously at the bent fender of the last car in the line.

At the next corner, Wentworth swung sharply away from the funeral, doubled twice and left the car standing. He abandoned his uniform cap, and bare-headed, strode to a subway entrance. When he reached his apartment at the Ritz-Carlton, the door was opened with slow stateliness by a Hindu clad all in white—long, loose trousers, an over-jacket like a smock that came almost to his knees, bound in close at the waist by a blood-red scarf. The man's head was wrapped in a white turban and his feet were bare. He bowed, touching cupped hands to his forehead. "Welcome home, *sahib,*" he murmured, and there was a flash of glistening white teeth.

Wentworth smiled grimly. "Thank you, Ram Singh. Is there any news?"

Ram Singh bowed again, "A certain Toussaints Louvaine phoned," he said. "He says he has news of utmost importance. He will phone again in ten minutes."

Wentworth frowned, pulling stern brows down over his eyes. The light went out of his face. Toussaints Louvaine would merely jeer at him, demand to know when he would locate the Lion Man, mouth more threats about Nita. Damn him! That man best beware! Wentworth walked unseeingly into the quietly expensive drawing room of his suite and began to pace up and down the floor. His hands were knotted behind him, his eyes on the floor.

It was past noon now. He had been without sleep for nearly sixty hours, without food since early morning.

"Master Dick!" Wentworth whirled. It was old Jenkyns, his face worried above the tea-table he rolled forward. On its spotless napery was spread a lunch. Wentworth was about to wave it aside; then he shrugged, flung himself into a chair, permitted Jenkyns to serve him. He ate hurriedly and with a distracted air.

When the telephone rang, he fairly leaped across the room to answer it himself. It was Professor Brownlee, reporting on his visit to Jones' home.

Wentworth listened dully. He didn't really expect any information from Jones. "That's fine," he said. "Yes, go ahead and do that and I'll check with you later."

HE HUNG up and paced back and forth the length of the room, his eyes flicking continually to the clock set upon a white, marble mantel. What could be delaying Louvaine? The ten minutes were past. It was nearly twenty minutes since Wentworth had entered the suite. He checked his stride, fighting his self-torture with a set, expressionless face, hands clenched at his sides. He had spent more than twelve hours in a pursuit that had ended in a blind alley. True, he could start all over again, go back to fire headquarters and await another lightning alarm. But hereafter, the collection men would be more careful. He had tipped his hand by his destruction of the four on First Avenue.

Should he go after Louis Baum, from whom Aronk Dong's men had collected, and try to force the truth from him? Should he go to Fulton Haybred and… Wentworth slammed a clenched fist into the palm of his left hand. Why hadn't he thought of Haybred before? Nothing had been destroyed as yet for which Haybred would need to pay. He must, then, have something that would be destroyed in the future. *The new skyscraper!*

By the heavens, that was it! McCorson had been beating Haybred to business, had wrested this latest contract from his hands almost at the last moment. It was the first really profitable undertaking in steel that had been begun in the city since the completion of the Empire State Building. And McCorson had to meet a contract deadline or lose high forfeit-money. It would ruin him if lightning blasted the already towering steel skeleton.

Wentworth strode to the telephone, plucked it up to call Kirkpatrick—to have him throw a guard about the structure. Then he hesitated. A daring plan flashed through his mind. On such a structure, only one means of attack could prevail. The Lion Man would loose one of his doom balloons, let it drift downward against the structure. If he could thwart the attack and force the Lion Man to come after him before he could fulfill his contract to destroy the skyscraper, then indeed Wentworth would have a lead to the Lion Man's hideout!

A bell buzzed and Wentworth started. He still held the phone in his hand and the operator had signaled him. He lifted the instrument to his ear.

"Richard Wentworth speaking," he said.

"Toussaints Louvaine!" an accented voice replied. "We've a lead to that party you are interest in. We've arrange for 'im to do a certain piece of work, as you suggest'. The rest is in your 'ands."

Wentworth hesitated, frowning down at the black orifice of the mouthpiece. "You attend to it!" he snapped. "I have another lead on which I am working."

Louvaine's voice sharpened. "No, no, Wentworth! This is your task. May I mention that I am in a position to exac' certain penalties?"

"At your own risk!"

Toussaints Louvaine laughed. "A car will call for you in fifteen minutes," he announced. "I advise that you enter it!"

CHAPTER 13
A DUEL OF THE MIGHTY

L OUVAINE WAS not in the Renault sedan that called for Wentworth. But after some involved doubling, during which the driver made sure they were not followed, the car stopped at a drug store and the trim, wry Frenchman stepped in. He lifted his left hand, with its twisted little finger, to the brim of his silk hat in a sardonic salute.

"I am very glad, *m'sieur,* that you are so promp'!"

"What are the plans?"

Toussaints Louvaine raised his brows. There was a sly jeer on his lips, but he met Wentworth's direct burning gaze—and he did not utter the jeer.

"En deux mots—" he said, "in two words, it's this: we have contract with Aronk Dong to destroy a certain tenement building. His collection man come for the firs' payment within the hour. I wis' you to—shall we say—receive 'im?"

Wentworth smiled and there was a wolfish twist to his lips.

"I shall not receive him," he stated flatly. "You will do that and I shall wait outside. I shall know then what to do."

Louvaine attempted to argue, but Wentworth ignored his arguments. Louvaine ceased urging, turned to threats. Then Wentworth's gray-blue eyes—like glacial ice—burned at him, and the Frenchman dismissed the whole matter with a shrug. He indicated the office where the collection man would come, and a cunning glint came into his small, black eyes.

"But there shall be certain ones," he warned, "who will see that you perform no treachery."

Wentworth answered with the same wolfish grin. He dropped from the Renault and once more took his stand to wait for the arrival of one of Aronk Dong's collection men.

It was an hour before the collection man came in a coupé that was twin to those that had been smashed in the battle on First Avenue. The sight of it stirred Wentworth's lips in a hard smile. Impatience quivered in his muscles. There was an excited thrumming in his blood. Never had he felt so ready for battle, so ready to kill and destroy these vermin who despoiled the earth. He turned the smile to a frown. He remembered he must not kill. He must only capture the Lion Man—for this sardonic Frenchman with dapper mustache and wry, thin neck which should be wrung like a chicken's!

The collection man left again and Wentworth pursued in a light coupé he had rented. He trailed cleverly but with impatience growing steadily in his breast until his heart beat in high tumult. Time and again his hand strayed to the gun butts beneath his arms, brushed the cigarette lighter in his vest pocket, whose base contained the seal of the Spider.

The chase was twisting, but it was not difficult. It seemed to Wentworth, almost as if the car ahead waited at times to make sure that he did not lose the trail. He told himself that was foolish, but the thought tightened his eyes. Was it possible that Louvaine had bribed the man ahead of him to lead the way? But he doubted that the Frenchman's avarice would have allowed him to waste money so. Then, why would he have…?

Wentworth ceased to wonder as the car drew to a halt before an apartment house in the upper east Eighties. The collection man sauntered into the building. There was a careless insolence to the fellow's bearing that thinned Wentworth's nostrils in anger. This was the sort of egocentric criminal whom the Spider had pledged his life to destroy.

WENTWORTH JERKED his coupé to a halt and strode openly toward the doorway of the apartment house. He was aware that the day had grown close and hot, that the sun no longer beat down on the pavement. With a curse, he jerked his eyes toward the skies and saw that in the South, dark clouds were piling up. Wentworth strode into the doorway toward the two elevators. Both doors slammed open and a machine gun gaped at him from each. Men rushed from the hallways to each side, a dozen of them, with leveled automatics. They ran forward with glinting eyes, with contemptuous smiles on their lips, but they did not fire. That was a mistake.

Wentworth flung a swift glance to each side and realized suddenly why the man he had trailed had delayed at the more complicated corners to make sure that Wentworth rode his trail. He had led the Spider into a trap and Wentworth knew abruptly that it had been intentionally that Toussaints Louvaine had set him upon this path. But before, Louvaine had wanted him to live; at least until the Lion Man could be found.

There was only one explanation of Louvaine's shift in attitude. He had found the Lion Man and now wished to be rid of Wentworth. Or Aronk Dong, knowing Wentworth and the Spider were one, had demanded his death as a price for opening negotiations to sell the Frenchman the secret of his lightnings. That was the more probable, since Louvaine had sent him into this trap rather than kill him in the Renault.

Wentworth tossed back his head and laughed. He threw the sound into the face of the killers like a challenge and, walking quite slowly, moved toward the machine gunner in the right-hand cage. They let him do that. Why shouldn't they? Could he walk faster than their bullets?

Four, five, six paces forward Wentworth walked while the gangster waited, gloating. Wentworth paused, faced them. His face convulsed with sudden rage. "Fools!" he snarled. *"I am the Spider!"*

As he hurled that stupefying phrase into their faces, hoping the news of the resurrection would stun them as it had stunned the detective on the streets, his hands flashed to his under-arm guns. The right gun he did not draw. He fired it backward through his coat into the breast of the machine gunner behind him. With the speed of Aronk Dong's own lightnings, he leaped backward into the elevator, snatching the machine gun from the dying hands of the man who gripped it.

The gangsters came to life. Their automatics hammered and slammed in the narrow corridor, choking it with a fury of sound. Wentworth, behind the double metal of the open doors, lifted the machine gun and poked its snout around the edge of his shield. He squeezed the trigger and the stammer of its explosions drowned out the other guns. Men's screams turned hoarse. Wentworth stepped into the open doorway and swung the nozzle of his bullet-hose back and forth across the lobby. Bodies jerked and crimsoned beneath the spray, but they no longer screamed.

The second machine gunner had stepped clear of the elevator to loose his hell weapon and he lay also amid the weltering shambles.

WENTWORTH TOED the body of the first machine gunner he had slain from the elevator. He stooped and affixed his red spider seal on the pale forehead; then he sent the cage upward. At each floor, he paused, but no sound save frightened cries came to him on any floor. And no one challenged him. If Aronk Dong were here… Wentworth left the machine gun in a porter's closet on the top floor. Thoughtfully, he disguised his features before he descended again to the first floor. He stepped out of the elevator into a circle of police, looked into the muzzles of their guns with an amused smile and a lift of his eyebrows. The policemen were white-faced, nauseated by the slaughter. In his rage, it left Wentworth unmoved. Apparently they had not yet found the Spider seal. When they discovered his resurrection and revealed it to the newspapers, the press would scream with the news. More than a dozen slain! Yes, it was a fitting return—a wholesome warning to the underworld.…

Wentworth nodded jauntily to the sergeant of police. "I see that some criminals have run afoul of justice," he drawled.

The sergeant gaped at him. Wentworth sauntered to the outer door and the officer recovered himself.

"Hey, you!" he bellowed.

Wentworth ducked out of the door, sprang into his coupé and spun away down the street. A policeman's gun racketed behind him. When he had turned the corner, he heard sirens. He turned another corner, alighted from the coupé and strolled on. He had slain before, but rarely with such fearful, direct carnage. A dozen men mowed down by machine gun bullets. He turned into a corner bar and downed two drinks of whiskey.

As he set down his glass the second time, he heard a distant rumbling mutter. Suddenly he remembered the threatening skies and the mounting clouds. He had reckoned for an accounting with Toussaints Louvaine, but that must wait. The skyscraper! That was his one true lead, after all. A thunderstorm was racing on the wings of death toward the city. The Spider must go forth to battle with the lightnings—with the fiend who directed them against the earth, Aronk Dong!

CHAPTER 14
BATTLE ON STEEL

WENTWORTH STRODE alertly from the saloon, pushing out through the doors hastily. There was movement on both sides and he leaped forward strongly, whirling in the air, snatching for his guns. He saw then that his assailants were two men—two scrawny rat-faced men, *Apaches* of Paris. Not content with sending Wentworth into a death trap, Toussaints Louvaine had sent his killers to make sure of the job!

The two *Apaches* were close upon him, slim, glittering knives held low against their thighs as they leaped in. Wentworth knew well the danger of those long, thin blades. That scar upon his right temple had come from such a knife in the hands of a man such as these. All these thoughts came while he was getting his first glimpse of the two, while his hand snaked toward his automatics. But there was no time to draw. He saw in the tensing arm of the *Apache* to his right that the man was ready to throw the knife.

The blade seemed no more than a flitting beam of light. Wentworth's left arm moved so rapidly that its outline blurred. There was a thump, then steel rang loudly on concrete. Guttural French snarled from the two men. And now the second *Apache* was upon him, ducking in low, blade sweeping up toward the groin. Wentworth's right hand shot out—not a fist—with fingers forked as a man would fork the head of a snake. His palm smacked on the back of the stooping man's neck, throwing him off balance. The blade swept up and missed Wentworth's recoiling body by a scant inch. He sprang to the right and now, finally, his guns leaped clear. On his knees, the second *Apache* jerked back his knife to throw.

Wentworth's right gun blazed and the man's body swayed on bent knees, head jerking back between his shoulders. At the close range, his forehead was shattered by the impact of the heavy caliber bullet. His companion was darting for the saloon door, hands thrown out before him in the desperate panic of his flight.

"This for you, Louvaine!" Wentworth muttered.

His bullet drilled the second man from side to side, smashed through lungs and heart. The body smacked down and the head crunched against the side-post of the door. Swiftly Wentworth crossed to the two men and affixed upon the forehead and a cheek of each the sinister seal of the Spider! Then he was away, streaking down the street on sprinting feet, knees flung high, head back. His guns were beneath his arms again.

He spun a corner, dropping to a quick walk even as he went around. A taxi-driver was jumping from his cab to peer about the corner at the excitement. Wentworth walked straight toward him.

"Forty-fifth and Second!" he ordered.

THE TAXI sped eastward, skipped across Broadway with a lucky change of lights. A thick mass of people was crowded into the open squares of the two triangles where Broadway and Seventh Avenue intersected at an oblique angle—a small open space where they hoped lightning would not strike. But suppose it smashed the towering steel and stone of the Times Building? Autos streamed northward toward the open greenery of Central Park. Street cars going that direction were swarmed. Some frenzied souls had even scrambled up on the top. The sky had become dark with blue-black clouds. Livid flashes of lightning snaked across the thunderheads and the rumbling concussions in the sky made the entire city shiver.

The taxi ground to a halt and the driver barely waited to be paid before he slammed into gear and raced northward.

Wentworth stared upward at the clouds; but not to gauge the lightning. There, against the blackness, reared the blue-black, towering steel, the new Gage Building which McCorson was erecting. Forty-five stories upward it had risen already. The stone facing had crawled up to the fifth floor. Wentworth saw the workers dropping hurriedly from the peak, elevators plunging, derricks lowering huge clots of men on their hooks like swarming bees.

He swung rapidly up the Avenue toward the North, nodded curtly when Ram Singh stepped from the Lancia and salaamed. "You got the incendiary bullets all right?"

"Han sahib!"

Wentworth motioned to the car and climbed in, glancing once more toward the towering steel skeleton. As yet, no slinking gray balloons scudded across the sky with their flashing death. Ram Singh sent the car forward smoothly and Wentworth picked up the speaking-tube mouthpiece.

"I am going up on the steel," he said quietly, "to shoot down the balloons as fast as I spot them. Unless I miss my guess, Aronk Dong will attempt to dislodge me

Wentworth swung the machine gun. Bodies fell before the spray of lead!

from my perch. I will attend to the fighting. It will be your task to capture one of the men and force him to tell where we can find the Lion Man. Or, failing in that, to follow one of them."

"*Wah, sahib!*" Wentworth could guess at Ram Singh's distaste for his task. "Is there no way thy servant can also join in the battle?"

"No, fearless one," Wentworth told the Hindu with a faint smile on his lips. "One other thing," Wentworth continued softly. "I recognized the garage from which Toussaints Louvaine rented his Renault. Phone there and perhaps you can locate him. Here is a message to deliver: Jackal traps will not hold a man of valor. They only anger him. Take care lest you anger him too much!"

Wentworth caught up a cardboard suit-box from the floor. It was heavy. He rested it against his hip as he alighted beside the skyscraper of the Gage Building. The Lancia pulled away and Wentworth pushed against a stream of men in overalls who were scrambling through the gate in the high board fence that surrounded the lower part of the structure. The faces of these girder-flies were white and frightened. Their eyes were strained wide and they saw nothing except the way to escape from danger.

A guard blocked the gate. Wentworth showed the police courtesy-badge which Kirkpatrick had given him.

"That's okey, buddy," the guard said, "but there's a storm rolling up. Lightning...."

Wentworth nodded gravely. "Quite so! The lightning is what brings me here. Will you have a man run me up on the lift?"

The guard gaped at him, then shrugged, hurried toward an engineer who was quitting his steam platform. "Run this nut up," he grunted.

The engineer broke into a torrent of obscenity. "I'm getting out of here before this whole damned thing comes down on me shoulders!" He grabbed a coat and started for the gate. Wentworth exposed his right hand and its gun almost apologetically.

"I'll have to trouble you to remain a few minutes," he said calmly. He could sympathize with the engineer. The lightning was crackling closer. Above them was a tower of bare steel, a natural attraction for lightning. Wentworth knew these things, and there was a high, slow throbbing of his heart at recognition of the danger. His voice cracked harshly. "Hop to it!"

THE ENGINEER jumped at the stern command in Wentworth's voice. His eyes swung to those of the Spider and he sprang to the levers. "And if you stop the cage before it reaches the top," Wentworth warned grimly, "I'll come around to see you tomorrow."

"You ain't gonna be here tomorrow," the engineer swore, but it was a mutter swallowed up in a crashing discharge from the skies. Wentworth mounted the open-sided lift and it lurched skyward. Within moments, he was above the lower, already brick-walled floors. Instantly, the sweep of the wind was upon him. It snatched at his coat, whipped it against his thighs. He leaned backward, tugged his hat down over his brows.

The street shrank to a narrow line. People became scurrying insects. He was flashing upwards now through an open lattice-work of steel. The wind threatened to fling him from the narrow, unguarded platform of the lift. Finally, with a lurch, the wooden platform halted. Wentworth peered upward. He was at the top of the shaft, but two spidery steel stairways above him. He scrambled to a straight walkway of planks thrown across the angle of two horizontal steel beams. Then he bent over his cardboard box.

The box opened to Wentworth's swift fingers and he snatched up a Thompson sub-machine gun, clapped a drum of bullets into place. He flung a swift look up-wind. No balloons yet, but the Lion Man would not delay long. With the machine gun cuddled against his hip, his left arm carrying his spare drums of ammunition, Wentworth stepped out on a beam and walked up-wind. The gusts jerked and pushed at him, pushing him back on his heels one moment, and the next, letting him plunge forward almost without resistance. Beneath his feet was a beam of steel twelve inches wide. And on each side lay nearly eight hundred feet of empty space…!

The flashes of the lightning were hot blows in his face, half-blinding him. He knew an instant of panic dread. Suppose, against the white-blue dazzle of the electrical outbursts he were not able to see the balloons when they came? He was in the spot where they must strike. Through him and past him would rush all the terrific discharge of power… The Lion Man would rage, unchecked.

The blue sparks were fat now and between the rumbling complaints of the thunder, Wentworth could hear their crisp crackling. His breath quickened. Fresh, clean-smelling air was all about him. A tiny thread of blue began to glitter along the barrel of the machine gun. And then he saw the balloon!

AGAINST THE dark gray lowering of the clouds, it was no more than a moving segment of a churning sky. It bubbled upward near the express highway which ran along the shore of the Hudson. It rushed toward the steel skeleton on the wings of the wind. Wentworth hitched his body to the left and concentrated on keeping the balloon in sight until it was close enough to fire upon. He squeezed the trigger of his gun, blasted a short burst into the wind and watched the lead's flaming course.

The balloon was lifting slowly, held back by the drag of the wire it trailed, but it was clear that it would pass cleanly above the skyscraper unless Wentworth interfered. And with the flail of its trailing wire, this structure would be smashed into bent junk.

The balloon was a hundred yards away now, sweeping on at high speed. At what point should he attempt to down it? Even after his incendiary bullets ripped through the gas envelope, the balloon might drift on. Better try it now....

As he swung up the muzzle of the sub-machine gun, the skies seemed to split wide open in a terrific blast of lightning and thunder that half-dazed Wentworth. His eyes were blinded, filled with dancing points of light. A hoarse curse rasped from Wentworth's lips. He could not see the balloon! It would be hard enough to hit that bobbing target in the face of this howling wind, even if it were plainly visible... But to strike it when he could only guess where it was... That was impossible! And the balloon must be within fifty yards by now, sweeping closer!

The balloon vanished in a
puff of flame and smoke!

Frantically, with narrowed eyes, he swept the sky again. There it was! Scarcely twenty-five yards away, bobbing high, dancing in the wind….

Wentworth threw the bullets at the balloon and he went blind in another, fierce lightning-crash. Peering with dazzled eyes, he sought to learn whether he had swept the gun-fire true, even through the crashing blast of the lightning.

For moments, he could see nothing at all. Then a speck of red that became a smear spotted the blue-black clouds.

Wentworth leaned weakly back against the steel girder laughing a high, cracked laugh. The balloon had vanished in a puff of flame and smoke—the remnants plunged downward, snatched from the sky by the weight of the dragging wire.

That was the first of the balloons. Wentworth shot down three more before the storm burst with a shattering hammer of rain that sluiced over him like a waterfall. He shielded the ammunition with his coat and waited. He had only one drum left. For the moment, at least, he had blocked Aronk Dong in his attack.

Twisting his head, he stared downward through the stilts of steel toward the earth. He could see it only mistily in the dense rain, but he thought that he detected movement, darkly blurred figures. He was positive that the Lion Man would keep watch on his balloons to make sure they accomplished their purpose. The very fact that four, instead of only one, had been released was evidence of that. He could not have failed, furthermore, to spot the streaking flames of the bullets that destroyed his balloons. Yes, Aronk Dong would attack!

ACROSS THE width of the building through the already

thinning rain, Wentworth saw the wooden platform of the elevator sink earthward. Down-wind from him, it made no audible sound. Moving at first slowly, it began to drop like a plummet before it had descended three floors. A faint squealing of rope blocks now came to him. The attack was under way! Slowly, soggily, but with an inward elation, Wentworth got to his feet, shifted to the other side of the vertical beam against which he had leaned. This way, he would have a clearer, uninterrupted view of the elevator. Carefully he strapped the machine gun to the pillar. The bullets were too precious to waste on men. He must save them for the balloons that might come later.

The squeak of a fall-block in the elevator came to him clearly and he saw that the ropes were moving swiftly, dragging the platform aloft once more. Wentworth waited until the men were only ten stories below him, then sent three automatic shots whistling down toward them.

"Throw down your guns!" he shouted, "or I'll shoot you full of incendiary bullets. They'll burn after they get inside of you. Throw them down, I say!"

The elevator continued to streak upward. There were three men on the platform. They crouched low, began firing. Bullets buzzed, clanged on steel and ricocheted shrilly into space. Wentworth gauged the elevator's rise carefully and fired twice. One of the men lunged to his feet with a strangled scream. He lurched, lost his balance and pitched headlong into the air. His shriek came back thinly. His clothing fluttered about him; then he disappeared into the blackness of the foundations. There was a great, smashing clatter of boards.

The elevator halted suddenly, two stories below Wentworth, and the two remaining men scrambled to the protection of steel beams, crouching low behind uprights. They could see Wentworth now, silhouetted black against the sky, and their lead began to reach for him. A bullet twanged off the beam on which he sat, but he made no move to change his situation. He was still pretty well protected and to shift his position would be to expose himself further. Besides, if he were hit while seated this way, he still had a chance. If he were standing when the bullet struck, he would be hurled to oblivion.

Wentworth snapped a swift shot downward as one of the gunmen dodged away from the elevator shaft, attempting to get in a better position to drop him. He had caught only a momentary glimpse of the gunman and there was no chance to aim. He simply snapped a shot, depended on his long practice to guide the bullet straight. Consequently, instead of striking a vital spot, he wounded the hood's arm. But that was enough! The man swayed on the edge of a beam, his arms waving in wide, frantic circles. Cries bellowed hoarsely from his lips. The third gunman darted from hiding, sliding ahead one foot at a time, along the beam on which his pal balanced. But he was still three feet away when, with a shrill despairing cry, the other gangster took the last, long dive.

"Stand still," Wentworth shouted while the man screamed his way earthward. "Unless you want to take a dive too, stand still!"

The second gangster was crouched over his gun. Wentworth

clanged a bullet off the steel at his feet. "Drop that gun!" he ordered.

FOR A space of fifteen seconds the man hesitated. Then, as lead whickered past him again, he tossed the gun wide and let it plunge downward.

"Good!" Wentworth commended quietly. "Now come up here where I am, and be damn quick about it."

The man cowered on the beam where he stood, clung with arms and legs wrapped about it. Under the stress of excitement, he had walked out on that thin bridge over nothingness, but now that the incentive was gone, he dared no longer move.

"I can't!" he whimpered. "If I move, I'll fall!"

Wentworth laughed aloud. He had accomplished what he planned—captured one of the Lion Man's henchmen alive. And the fellow was nailed to that beam as effectively as if bound there.

"For God's sake," the captive screamed, suddenly. "Look behind you! A balloon!"

Wentworth wrenched about, saw the bulging destruction-carrier drifting toward him. The air was quieter now and the balloon made a more nearly stable target as it rose slowly into the sky, dragging its dread, charged wire toward the structure Aronk Dong wanted to demolish.

Wentworth reached around the pillar, slid the machine gun back into his lap. His third burst sent the balloon down in flames. After that, he strode along a steel beam to a wooden ladder that led down, while the gangster below stared up with a dead-white, terrified face. To him, this man striding with scornful ease along that twelve-inch walkway of steel, ignoring the depths into which two men had already plunged to their deaths, seemed almost godlike. This man had blasted down the Lion Man's balloons five times as they rose to wreak destruction. And now, this man was on the same level with himself, striding toward him along the beam, a machine gun held carelessly in his hand.

"Help me!" the gangster begged weakly.

Wentworth stopped and looked down at the gunman. He reached out a foot and carelessly prodded him. The gangster screamed, clung desperately while Wentworth laughed.

"I take it you don't want to take the dive?" he said.

"For God's sake, no!" the man gasped.

"You're going to," Wentworth promised slowly, "unless you give me some information about the Lion Man."

A whimpering moan was choked out of the hood. He laid his face down on the steel beam and wept. "I can't do that! I can't!" he groaned. "Aronk Dong would tear me to pieces with his claws. He'd point his finger at me and lightnings would kill me! Or he'd turn me over to that Chink of his to play with. For God's sake, don't make me talk about Aronk Dong!"

Wentworth crouched on the steel beam, straddled it. He kicked gently at the man's dangling legs. Incoherent babblings came from the gangster. He clutched still more frantically at the steel. Wentworth was frowning as he went about forcing the man to talk. These were new things he was learning about Aronk Dong. He had some mechanical trick of electrocuting a man by pointing his finger. And this Chinese, too, was new. Wentworth's prisoner was terribly frightened, yet his dread of

Aronk Dong was greater than his dread of plunging into space. Wentworth's face hardened. He would soon determine how far the fear of Aronk Dong would carry.

Deliberately, he kicked the man's right thigh in such a way that the leg was paralyzed. The hood's ankles unlocked and his legs dangled limply. Wentworth reached forward with his gun, slashed at the man's right bicep. The arm, too, came loose, dangled. The gangster was screeching like a soul in torment.

"Shall I paralyze your other arm and leg also?" Wentworth asked softly. "Or will you talk?"

"I can't! *I can't!*" It was a heartbreaking scream. "You can't throw me off! You can't!"

THE MOCKING, flat laughter of the Spider sounded strange there, high up in the thin air. Wentworth reached forward and struck the man's left bicep so that arm was numb and weak, too. The gangster was no longer holding on. He was simply lying on the beam, held there by his weight and nothing more. A stifled moan came from the Lion Man's henchman. After that, there was no sound at all except his heavy, rasping breathing. He lay utterly still, cheek pressed flat to the beam. The heavy storm-clouds had passed away now, and in the West, the sky was turning a brilliant gold. Its light made the man's face more ghastly—emphasized the white panic that ravened him. His eyes were clamped shut.

"This is your last chance!" Wentworth cautioned slowly, his voice deep. "I am going to ask you a question. If you do not answer it, I'm going to *push you off!* A servant of Aronk Dong who will not talk for me is better dead." He reached forward and caught hold of the man's belt, felt a shudder tremble over him. "Here is the question: Where is Aronk Dong?"

For seconds, the man did not move, but lay there panting heavily. Wentworth tightened his hold on the man's belt.

"All right!" The man's voice was squeezed out, strangled. "I'll talk! The louse was going to kill me with that balloon. I'll talk. He's over in the…."

His body jerked convulsively, and there was a thump of metal digging into flesh. He shivered, and as Wentworth jerked his hand free, staring about wildly, the gangster sighed flutteringly, toppled, and shot downward. From far off, came the thin, whip-like crack of a rifle. With the sound, Wentworth flung face down on the steel beam, jerked himself forward with his hands. Only for a second did he remain in that posture. He got to his feet, took two swift strides. Then he stopped dead.

Through the thin air just ahead of him, a rifle bullet *screeed*. Wentworth bent double, took four long strides forward, dropped flat and crawled. Above his head, another bullet whined, and far off again came the dim crack of the rifle.

Abruptly, Wentworth checked his advance, thrust himself backward a full yard. Lead clanged on the steel and instantly he was on his feet. He did not halt, or change pace again, but sprang for the steel pillar that rose above his head. He made it even as the sullen *ping* of another bullet plucked at him.

Once more, death had cheated him of information! But this time, the very agency that saved Aronk Dong would work against him. Those rifle shots were coming from the direction of the river and upward. In that direction was a freight terminal, the only high structure. But it would take Wentworth long, precious minutes to climb down the ladders to the floors below, minutes in which that long-distance sniper could peck continually at him. And in the meantime, Aronk Dong might flee. The Spider had no way of telling how long the Lion Man would stay there. It might be only a spot from which he released the balloons and fled immediately.

Swiftly, Wentworth whipped off his coat. He shoved the machine gun to his back. Then, wrapping his coat around his forearms and hands, he sprang out into space and seized the wire cables that operated the elevator. For a half-dozen floors, he shot downward in an almost unchecked gravity fall. Then he began to put pressure on the coat with which he gripped the rope. He braked himself on the cable with his shoe soles. It was only for an instant; then he was shooting downward again. Here, too, he must "change pace," lest that distant sniper gauge his speed, and blast him into space....

THE WIND shot upward around him. His clothing fluttered with the speed of his plunge. If lead whined past, he did not hear it. He was more than halfway down now. He must check his speed again. He put pressure on his hands, wrapped in the coat. The wire cable tore at the garment. His arms shot straight up over his head, and for an instant, the rope brushed his shirt. The fine broadcloth was stripped from his body, torn to fluttering shreds that whipped by his face. But his speed was noticeably checked. He increased the pressure slowly, touched tentative shoes against the wire. He flashed into the darkness of the interior of the building, gripped harder still, and spilled to the ground with a force that almost dazed him. He reeled to his feet a little groggily, climbed out of the shaft pit. Ram Singh ran to help him. The Hindu's face was grim and worried.

"*Wah, sahib!*" he exclaimed. "I am no fighter, but an old woman! I had to kill the man they left below. I could not capture him alive."

Wentworth swept his hand in a sharp, forgiving gesture. "The car, quickly!" He ran toward it beside the Hindu, swung into the back as Ram Singh leaped to the driver's seat.

"Huber Freight Terminal, due west!" Wentworth snapped.

The Lancia fairly sprang forward. Wentworth eased the strap of the machine gun, swung it around in his lap. He became conscious of his shredded shirt and, with a tight smile, he reached under the left-hand cushion and pressed a button. The seat slid forward, revolving as it moved, and revealed a neatly hung wardrobe in its back. From it, the Spider selected a sweater and drew it swiftly over his head. He reloaded his automatics, thrusting them inside his belt against the hard muscles of his stomach. He drew a cap down on his brows.

The freight terminal was only a block away, now, along streets which the terror of the storm had cleared of all persons. Wentworth leaned forward to tap on the glass to have Ram Singh stop and saw a frosty, round patch blossom on the windshield, heard the crack of a rifle! An instant later, the Lancia lurched heavily, swerved toward the curb with a hiss of air. The windshield was bullet proof, but the tires were not.

His teeth glinting between drawn-back lips, Wentworth

lifted the machine gun into his lap. He had only part of a drum of ammunition left, but....

"You have your gun, O warrior?" he called to the Hindu.

"Han, sahib!" Ram Singh agreed. He lifted a blue-black automatic into view above the seat back. "Do we attack?"

Wentworth laughed softly. "Don't fire until you see the whites of their eyes!"

Two more bullets pecked at the bullet proof glass, leaving frosty stars on it, but Wentworth made no attempt to retaliate. He had small ports in the glass that could be opened when he wished to fire, but for the present, he was satisfied to wait... There was little danger of outside interference. Police had ducked to cover from the lightnings, even as had the people. Wentworth whistled softly between his teeth. He was sure now that he had been in time to intercept Aronk Dong before the Lion Man could leave the freight terminal. And the Spider was ready. True, he was sealed in a car by watching, vengeful killers....

With a harsh curse, Wentworth leaned sharply forward. Backing around the corner just ahead was a wrecking car of the type garages use, a powerful stub derrick at the back. And in the rear of the truck, behind an armored shield, crouched a man with a machine gun. He made no attempt to fire, but watched alertly while the truck backed up into a position to fasten to the front of Wentworth's car. Once that was accomplished, they could carry the Lancia and its two occupants anywhere they wished.

"Wah, sahib!" Ram Singh's voice was low and tense. "Shall we attack *now?*"

Wentworth leaned back in his seat quietly. He fondled the machine gun. His eyes glittered.

"No, Ram Singh," he said. "I have an idea they will take us where we want to go—to see Aronk Dong!"

CHAPTER 15
FACE TO FACE

WENTWORTH CALMLY lit a cigarette while the gangsters derricked up the front of the Lancia and started to tow it away. Once that was accomplished, machine gunner and shield disappeared from the truck, but another car kept close to the Lancia's rear. Ready guns blocked escape. Ram Singh was tense as a hunting dog on the front seat.

"*Sahib!*" he called back softly. "Easily could I shoot a tire off that truck. You could open the rear window and with your machine gun...."

"No, Ram Singh!"

He saw the Hindu shift restlessly on his inclined seat and a smile lifted Wentworth's mouth corners. He blew smoke at the ceiling. Through days of death and destruction he had fought to contact the Lion Man. Now, at last, he was to achieve his wish. It was not the most ideal arrangement of course, but he had his weapons. In that secret compartment beneath the seat were hand-grenades and tear-gas bombs. The situation could easily be much worse.

For over an hour, the strange procession pushed steadily northward, loafing along upper Broadway, skimming past rows of monotonously similar apartment houses, roaring on into the open country. They turned finally from the main road into a narrow lane and the lounging springs of the Lancia rode Wentworth smoothly over vicious mud-holes. The truck stopped and the Lancia rocked gently, creaking on the derrick chain.

It was completely dark, except for the headlights of the cars. Presently light flashed on in a small house ahead; then a man with a leveled machine gun walked toward the Lancia. His voice was muffled by the thick glass.

"Get out!" he ordered. "And leave your weapons inside!"

Wentworth turned on the dome-light in the ceiling of the car's tonneau and smiled cheerily at the man outside. "I think I'll wait a while, if you don't mind!"

The man squeezed the trigger of his gun and lead hammered viciously on the bulletproof window, covering it with a crackled frosting as the outer layer absorbed the blows. If that continued, Wentworth knew, the glass would eventually go to pieces. He leaned forward, opened a small port in the armored door and fired one shot. The machine gun stuttered wildly for a few seconds more. Then it was still. Wentworth leaned back, peered through a part of the glass that was not cracked. The machine gunner lay writhing upon the ground.

"When Aronk Dong comes," Wentworth shouted, his voice beating back at him in the close space, "I'll leave the car! I won't leave before then. If any other man tries to dislodge me, that man will die!"

"I am here, Wentworth!" a deep voice boomed from the darkness. "Come out, or I'll blow you and the car to hell with my lightning!"

"Show yourself, Aronk Dong!" Wentworth jeered.

There was no answer from the darkness. Aronk Dong did not show himself; nor did any other of his men. The machine gunner upon the ground shuddered and lay still. Presently, fat, blue sparks of hell's lightning began to dance over the frame work of the car. Wentworth reached above his head and switched off the light. He was frowning and his heavy-lidded eyes were glistening with hate.

"Time to attack, O Ram Singh," he announced softly. "When I shoot at the headlights of the car behind us, turn on our own. We will go out together on opposite sides of the car."

"Han, sahib!" came the Hindu's swift response. *"Wah,* these men are as nothing! They are pigmy fighters who hide in the trees and shoot arrows at the eyes of elephants."

WENTWORTH RETORTED grimly, "Yes, and they kill the elephants. Get ready!" Wentworth whirled, flung open the rear port of the car and smashed out the headlights behind him. Instantly he was at the door, flinging it wide as he leaped clear with automatics thrust back into his belt, with the machine gun in his hands.

Wentworth's feet hit the ground and a stinging, numbing shock raced over him. He tried to shout a warning to Ram Singh. Then he felt his senses reel, felt his knees buckle. He slumped forward on his face, bowled over by an electric trap which Aronk Dong had arranged! The earth gripped him like a magnet. He heard Aronk Dong's booming laughter, was aware that the Lion Man strode forward toward him across the charged earth while others of his men hung back in fear.

"Did you think you could master *me*, Spider?" Aronk Dong jeered. "Puny earthworm, did you think you could out-think a man from Mars?"

Wentworth, helpless to resist, was flopped over on his back and stripped of all his weapons. Handcuffs were snapped on his wrists and the broad, swaggering shoulders of Aronk Dong retreated. He knew that Ram Singh was being similarly treated. The electricity was writhing torture. His senses were reeling when the current ceased.

He fought the weakness of muscles that refused to obey his will, rolled and staggered feebly to his feet. He stood on braced legs, half-conscious, and Aronk Dong came and stood before him again, leonine brows drawn down darkly over tawny eyes. There was a gleam of admiration there.

"You are quite a man, Spider!" his deep voice rumbled. "You have resisted my currents for five minutes and retained your senses."

He lifted a hand and five men ringed Wentworth with drawn guns and urged him, impotent and reeling, toward the house. He knew what was going on about him but he saw everything as through a haze of smoke. He saw Ram Singh carried up the steps and into the cottage, found his own way with numb, stumbling feet. He saw a girl staring at him with a white face and knew it was Bets Decker. He had a glancing thought that he had been right about Brandon Early's guilt. Then blackness enfolded him.

WENTWORTH CAME to suddenly with his head as clear as a bell. "That's fine," he heard Aronk Dong's rumbling, deep voice say. He was aware that hands had just finished massaging his neck. He snapped his eyes open, looked up into the cruel face of the Lion Man. "That's fine," the Man from Mars repeated. "I want you to see a little sample of Martian justice. Can you sit up?"

Wentworth sat up, found that his feet as well as his hands were snuggly bound. He was conscious of a queer physical elation and guessed that it was the result of some stimulant the Lion Man had injected to revive him. Wentworth was on the floor. He hunched backward, propped his back against a wall, glancing curiously about the room. It was empty except for three articles of furniture: two chairs and a table, all bolted to the floor. Both of the chairs were curiously connected with electric wires. But it was not at this that Wentworth looked. Against the right-hand wall of the room, six men stood, against another who was alone. The single man's forehead was beaded with sweat and his face had already the pasty whiteness of death.

"This man failed me," Aronk Dong pointed at the one who stood alone.

The man stiffened with a gasp as the Lion Man's finger indicated him, but he seemed utterly incapable of moving from the spot.

"He knows that he is doomed," Aronk Dong continued casually. "I have promised him a merciful death if he can take it like a man. You are grateful for that, aren't you, Patrick?" The Lion Man turned toward the wretched victim with a slow, cruel smile, his tawny eyes half-hidden by dropping lids. The man's jaw trembled and he swallowed twice but could not get words out.

"Aren't you, Patrick?" Aronk Dong purred again, more emphatically.

"Yes, Aronk Dong," the man gasped.

Aronk Dong nodded. "You see, he is brave. I reward him." Once more he pointed his index finger at the man. This time, blue sparks glittered at its tip. The man called Patrick stiffened with a frantic jerk, all his muscles tightening under the goad, apparently, of a powerful electric current. He leaped, as if effortlessly, six inches clear of the floor; then he slumped down in a shapeless heap. Twice more the spark glittered at Aronk Dong's finger tip and twice the corpse jerked convulsively. Then the Lion Man waved his hand. Fearfully, the six remaining men, white-faced as the victim, crept across the room, picked up the corpse and bore it from sight through a black doorway.

Wentworth felt rage quivering over him like an ague. But he made an effort to dissemble. He smiled up into the sleepy-eyed face of the Lion Man.

"So you have decided to be merciful to me?" he asked lightly. "Or have you devised some new process of death for the Spider?"

Aronk Dong brushed his heavy mustaches with their cat-bristles spiking out on each side. His sensual lips were stiffly curling.

"I know you are brave, Spider," he said casually, his deep voice rumbling like an echo of his own thunders, "but I am not certain just how brave. I am going to find out!"

He pointed a finger straight toward the ceiling. Blue sparks glittered at its tip. From a black doorway, a Chinese came forward on the silent feet of a cat. His face was dead except for glittering eyes. Wentworth saw that, like the Lion Man, he carried his fingers curled in upon themselves. Suddenly this slant-eyed celestial seemed strangely feline also.

"So you have Chinese on Mars?"

Aronk Dong nodded with amused eyes but volunteered no words. The Chinese seized Wentworth under the arms and dragged him to his feet. He did it with absurd ease, the strength of a derrick in his reed-like arms. He slid Wentworth into one of the chairs, fastened straps about him—a broad one across his chest, a narrow one about his throat—so that he could not lean forward an inch without strangling against it. Other straps went about his thighs and ankles, and a cold clasp of metal gripped him just above the calf. Throughout all that, Wentworth maintained his casual, quiet smile.

IT WAS impossible to tell what this creature planned for him, except that it was surely death.

Not only were his hands fastened together—he saw with a momentary frown that they were bound with rope now instead of fastened with handcuffs and wondered at the change—but he was strapped to a heavy, immovable chair. His arms were jerked forward abruptly and two more leather straps came into play, this time securing his wrists to the edge of the table. He could move them forward or back a few inches and that was all. Still Wentworth smiled.

"I can't help being a bit curious," Wentworth drawled carelessly. "Would it be against the rules of the game to ask the purpose of all this?"

"It would be against the rules," Aronk Dong agreed. He stalked across the room after the silent gliding figure of the Chinese; then he turned in the door to peer back at his prisoner.

"It might interest you to know, however," he said, "that shortly your friend, Kirkpatrick, will sit in the other chair, and that you two gentlemen will have a witness for the game you are going to play—none other than that charming lady, Nita van Sloan!"

Wentworth heard that without change of countenance. With a mocking grin, the Lion Man was gone. Wentworth waited until his footfall faded away entirely. Then he went to work systematically to test his bonds. While he wrenched and twisted, his mind seethed with the implications of that last statement the Lion Man had made. Nita would be here soon, and Kirkpatrick. How, in heaven's name, had the creature made that capture? It was clear about Nita, of course; Toussaints Louvaine had surrendered her. Wentworth was not sure but that he would rather have her in the Frenchman's hands. The kidnapping of the Commissioner of New York police was an astounding feat…!

But all that was beside the point. He must escape from these bonds or all of them would be doomed. Not only that, but the last obstacle restraining this hybrid demon would be removed. Unchecked, he could wreak his will upon the people, destroying and murdering. Frantically, Wentworth struggled against straps and ropes. It was futile. There was no give at all. There was a moment when Wentworth lost his calm, fought his bands until they tore his flesh. There was a moment when he barely checked back a despairing cry. Finally, he achieved calm again and sat smiling and casual, despite his helplessness. At least, the Spider knew how to die...!

CHAPTER 16
A TEST FOR THE BRAVE

WENTWORTH WAS like that, smiling and outwardly calm, when Kirkpatrick was marched in with bound hands a half-hour later. He said, very quietly, "Good evening, Kirk!"

Kirkpatrick's bitterly angry face had tightened with new rage at the sight of Wentworth so helplessly bound, but at his friend's pleasant greeting, he returned:

"How are you, Dick?"

Kirkpatrick was thrust forward, pinioned in the other chair. His arms were unbound and each one was strapped down to the arms of the chair, which terminated in bright electrodes. Wentworth had been too busy before to analyze the connections of the chair in which Kirkpatrick was now strapped as helplessly as himself. He realized with a shock that it was an electric chair such as was used in the death-house at Sing Sing. There was this difference: instead of a hood to drop over the condemned man's face, there was an electrode dangling from the ceiling which could be strapped to Kirkpatrick's head with a chin-tie.

When Kirkpatrick was securely fastened, Aronk Dong came through the door, escorting Nita. Behind him came a man bearing two light chairs, and a third man with still another. The men placed the chairs against the left wall in a single line, bound them together with a wire cable. Nita nodded cheerfully to Wentworth as she was led toward these lighter chairs and tied in them with elaborate lashings of rope.

The Lion Man bent over Nita's hands seriously. He nodded. "I think that will hold even the Spider's mate." He turned toward the door and gestured. Four men entered, bringing two more prisoners. Ram Singh was one, and—*Toussaints Louvaine!*

"Another failure," Aronk Dong waved his hand toward the Frenchman as the latest prisoners were lashed to chairs. "He failed to keep a bargain with me to deliver you into my hands, dead or alive. I was finally forced to do it myself." He smiled at Wentworth. "You didn't really think that all your foolish jumping up there on the steel beams kept my bullets from hitting you, did you?"

Wentworth nodded, with every outward sign of cheerfulness. "And I still think so!" he said gently.

Aronk Dong frowned. He tossed his head so that his great mane of reddish black hair fell back smoothly in a pompadour. "You are entitled to your belief," he growled savagely. "But whether you believe it or not, you will at least concede that it was the rifle shots that led you into my trap?"

"Oh, I suppose so," Wentworth agreed negligently. He turned his head from Aronk Dong to Nita. "This French rat didn't molest you in any way, dear?" he queried. "I promised him a quite painful death, if he did."

Nita shook her head and smiled.

"No!" she said in a low, even voice. "But he used me to trap

157

Kirk. He let me get to a phone and call Kirkpatrick. Then he carried me away. His *Apaches* killed five or six police."

"Seven," Kirkpatrick snarled savagely. "He shall answer to me personally for that."

ARONK DONG laughed boomingly. "It is as pleasant a party as I could have hoped," he chortled. "It may relieve you some to know, before you die, Mr. Kirkpatrick, that the *Apaches* are dead, too. I have enjoyed the bit of competition you gentlemen have provided, but I no longer wish to worry with you. I am more concerned right now with results!" He threw back his head, thumped himself resoundingly on the chest. "Tonight I take the first step toward conquering the world!"

He was glaring directly at Wentworth, and Wentworth lifted mocking brows at the beast. "Really?" he murmured.

Aronk Dong strode to the table, smashed his fist down upon it.

"Jeer all you wish!" he thundered. Then he caught himself, straightened and coaxed a small, stiff smile to his lips. "If you wish, Wentworth, you may live to see it. I have prepared a place for you."

"Excellent!" Wentworth was still murmuring. "And how do you propose to accomplish this conquest of the world?"

"Ver', ver' interestin'!" Toussaints Louvaine chimed.

Aronk Dong whirled with a curse, sprang toward the little Frenchman with his right hand drawn back to strike. Claws glittered like steel, but the Lion Man checked short of the blow. He stiffened, blowing out his breath hoarsely. Toussaints Louvaine laughed up into his face.

"Why not kill me?" Louvaine jeered. "I am bound and 'elpless. Free me and you woul' not dare be'ave in such fashion."

"I would not dare!" It was a howl. "Aronk Dong would not dare!"

The Lion Man took another mad stride toward the French-man, but once more he checked himself. There was an insane light in his eyes, but there was cunning there also. "No! No!" he cried. "I am saving you for the Spider!"

"Magnifique!" Louvaine jeered. "Such restrain'!"

Aronk Dong ignored him. "You ask how I plan to conquer the world, Wentworth, though of course you can guess the weapon I mean to use. What you want is more detailed information. I do not hesitate to give it to you. Tonight I shall destroy the water supply of New York City!"

Wentworth felt the smile fade off his face, felt the chilling fever of rage sing through his veins. It was a fiendish thing, yet simple to accomplish with Aronk Dong's lightnings. There were a half-dozen, huge, major reservoirs, and all their dams could be smashed within a space of minutes. Horror and panic would follow.

"Afterward," Aronk Dong went on, "I shall send my planes with loudspeakers all over the land, warning that unless the nation bows to me, I shall destroy the whole country the same way. I am the modern Attila. I shall rule the world!"

ARONK DONG raised his clenched fist above his head, and once more there was wild madness in his eyes. His voice roared, crowded the room with sound. Even the sneering Toussaints Louvaine seemed to feel the awfulness of the creature. Slowly the Lion Man calmed the heaving of his chest. His eyes fastened on Wentworth.

"There shall be a place for you in my plans!" he repeated, more softly. "You shall have your sweetheart free! You shall have your enemy—this French failure—on whom to wreak vengeance. Your servant will come back alive. All of these things are yours if you are brave enough!"

He took a gleaming knife from his belt, reached up to a wire that dangled from the ceiling and fastened it. Then he flung the knife, point down, so that it quivered in the table between Wentworth's hands.

"If you are brave enough to use that knife!" Aronk Dong roared.

Wentworth glanced swiftly up the wire leading from the knife handle. He saw that it led to the head electrode which now had been strapped to Kirkpatrick's skull.

"But I must warn you," Aronk Dong boomed, "that you must act quickly. This house is exactly in the path of Kanawba Dam. Within an hour, that dam shall be smashed by lightning and the flood waters will pour over this spot. If, by that time, you have not used the knife, you and your sweetheart, your servant and your enemy, will die together—not to mention Commissioner Kirkpatrick!"

Wentworth's eyes flicked from the knife to Aronk Dong and back again. He felt a tingling in the calf of his leg where the electrode was fastened and with dawning comprehension, he pulled his hands away from the knife gingerly.

"It would not hurt you, Wentworth, to touch the knife,"

Aronk Dong purred, "but it would electrocute your friend, Kirkpatrick. You see, I pass you a nice little problem in ethics and ask if you have the courage to solve it. If you touch the knife, killing your friend, you can free yourself. Perhaps you can even prevent me from destroying New York's water supply. Also, you can save your sweetheart's life.

"If you do not use the knife, you will all die here together within an hour.

"Which shall it be, Wentworth? The life of your friend, or the lives of thousands who will die in New York if you do not get free? I give you everything to live for, Wentworth, your sweetheart and your vengeance—if you will only kill your friend!

"A nice problem in ethics, eh, Spider?"

Aronk Dong flung back his head and laughed. He turned, walked out of the room and his laughter floated back, evil and gloating. Wentworth's eyes were fixed in a hypnotic stare at the knife. They lifted from it, trailed the wire to the electrode on Kirkpatrick's head.

"Go ahead, Dick," Kirkpatrick said quietly. "There can be but one choice. You must protect the people. Within the hour, we'll all be dead anyway. If you don't—touch the knife!"

Across the table, Wentworth stared into his friend's eyes. The faces of both men were dead white, but there was no weakness in the set of their lips.

"In your place," said Wentworth slowly, "I would say the same thing. But it is a much easier thing to die than to—to kill a friend."

Toussaints Louvaine laughed raucously. "A nice problem in

ethics!" he jeered. "But are you brave enough to solve it? I shall enjoy to see. Myself, I am neutral. Either way, *moi*, I die!"

"For God's sake, Dick, hurry," Kirkpatrick rasped suddenly. His lips twisted in what was meant for a smile. "It's inhuman to keep the condemned man waiting in the electric chair!"

CHAPTER 17
THE SPIDER IS BRAVE

WENTWORTH'S FISTS slowly knotted: his wrists swelled until the straps that bound his wrists to the table edge were bone-tight. He strained against the leather that held him. The band about his throat cut into the flesh and shut off his wind. His bonds creaked, held.

"It's useless," Kirkpatrick said, calm now. "Get it over with. You will need a whole hour even to try to defend the dams."

Wentworth relaxed in his bonds and panted for air that seemed to burn his throat. There must be a way out! Kill his friend; kill Kirkpatrick? God in heaven! He couldn't!

Kirkpatrick was talking again. "Listen, Dick," he said, "you have faced nearly this same problem before. Nita has been kidnapped and her life held hostage—and you fought on. This is no different. It would not be your hand that killed me, but Aronk Dong's. I know I should be avenged."

Wentworth laughed sharply. It was ridiculous, that Kirkpatrick should beg for death from his hand. He laughed again and his laughter threatened to break into madness. As Kirkpatrick said, why should he hesitate? He had made this decision often before this. He should act now, so that he would have the greatest possible time to thwart the Lion Man's plans. Forget that this was Kirkpatrick; consider it merely another life standing between him and victory over the Lord of the Lightnings. Forget that it was Kirkpatrick....

But it *was* Kirkpatrick, the man he had fought through months of criminal warfare, who later had become his ally against the underworld—the man whom above all others on earth he revered and respected. Why, damn it, they were *friends!*

"Quickly, Dick," Kirkpatrick urged. He threw all his will into his eyes, forced his stiff lips into a slight smile. "After all, life is a little thing. You and I are used to risking ours. Any day, any hour, we may stop a gangster's bullet. My fate happens to be an electric wire. And I am tired of struggling anyway. If you see pallor in my face, it is only this physical body that shrinks; it is not my inner self." He barked out an oath: "I wish to God that I could reach that knife!"

This was no problem in ethics. It was damnable soul torture. Wentworth's teeth locked; his breath hissed. His face was a white hating mask. He realized another thing. Aronk Dong had figured that even if Wentworth made the decision, killed his friend to attempt to save the city, his spirit would be gone. No longer would he be able to fight.

His eyes lifted once more to Kirkpatrick's face and his own jaw clamped until it ached. Kirkpatrick saw the decision in his eyes and brought a gentle smile to his lips. Never had Wentworth seen the kindliness of the man shine forth as at that minute when death at the hands of his friend confronted him.

"I knew you had courage. Dick," he said quietly. "It's the only way." Kirkpatrick drew a deep breath. "Get it over with, Dick. Good luck and good hunting! I wish I could shake your hand."

A smothered sob forced itself from Nita's lips. She strangled it swiftly, and neither man looked toward her. Toussaints Louvaine's breath was harshly audible.

Wentworth tore his eyes from Kirkpatrick, looked down at the knife before him, a half-inch of its point embedded sturdily in the wood. It had been shrewdly thrown. It was precisely where his bound hand could grasp it. He opened his clinched right fist, the fingers curling as if even his flesh rebelled at the thing his mind ordered. Abruptly, his eyes narrowed. He lifted his gaze to Kirkpatrick.

"Good bye!" he said tonelessly as he forced his wrist to bend toward the knife hilt. Kirkpatrick was not looking at the knife. He was gazing into his friend's face, still smiling. He was relaxed in his straps, in his death chair.

Then suddenly, Wentworth was leaning back weakly in his chair, laughing, wildly, almost hysterically.

"Quit it, Dick!" Kirkpatrick snapped. "Pull yourself together! Grab the knife!"

Wentworth shook his head. He felt almost incapable of movement. His voice was faint. He had come so near to murdering his friend—uselessly!

"Don't you see?" he shouted. "I don't have to touch the knife to cut my wrist ropes!"

KIRKPATRICK STARED at him incredulously, jerked his eyes to the arrangement on the table and cursed under his breath. It was true. Wentworth's wrists were so tied that he could cut the rope by rubbing them against the knife.

"Your wrists?" Kirkpatrick questioned, and his voice showed his effort against hope. "Your wrists, will they slide through the straps if the ropes are cut?"

"I don't know," Wentworth said tightly, "but I'm sure going to find out. Kirk, this will probably jolt you now and then. It may even knock you out, but I'm quite sure it will do no more than that."

He strained his wrists as far apart as possible. There was a two-inch gap between them, for Aronk Dong had intended to make it a simple matter for him to cut the ropes—once he grasped the knife. But two inches was perilously little. It meant that each wrist would be less than an inch from the steel blade. Carefully, carefully, gauging the distance with narrowed eyes, he shoved his wrists and the rope toward the knife. Nita was crying unrestrainedly now and a steady stream of curses poured from Louvaine's lips.

The tingling of the current began when Wentworth's wrists were still three inches from the knife. He glanced at Kirkpatrick, but saw no indication that he felt the pricking of the electricity. He pushed nearer. Two inches now and the veins were writhing in his own wrists. Small muscles jerked and quivered on the backs of his hands. Kirkpatrick was feeling it all right, his face twitching uncontrollably. With a curse, Wentworth rammed the rope against the blade.

The electrode burned his leg. His arms were tense, almost paralyzed with the grip of the current, but Wentworth ground his teeth together and by sheer will power forced them up the fraction of an inch the straps allowed, then down again. He could not move his hands fast. And the least movement was torture....

Kirkpatrick was straining against his straps, his face a tortured mask. From under the electrode on his head, a small, thick string of smoke twined upward. The odor of burning hair drifted nauseously across the room.

Frantically, Wentworth sawed at the ropes. One popped and he tugged outward with his wrists, drawing them a fraction of an inch further apart. He could not thrust too violently against the edge of the blade, lest he dislodge it from the wood and the whole battle be lost. He sawed back and forth, tediously, against the steel. Another rope sliced through, and once more his wrists drew a fraction further apart.

Wentworth cursed. He saw that, since the ropes had been made into manacles and knotted closely against his wrists, he would have to saw through every strand before his bonds would separate. But the swelling of his veins from the electrode lash had enlarged his arms now until his muscles were almost useless. Panting, exhausted, he pulled his wrists clear of the current and sank back in his chair. Kirkpatrick slumped in his bonds, head lolling. He lifted it with a brave effort and forced a smile to his lips.

"The worst of it is over, Kirk," Wentworth said stiffly. "Once more, not as bad as before, and my wrists will be free!"

While precious seconds slipped past, Wentworth and Kirkpatrick rested, eyes closed. A slow thought was forming in

Wentworth's brain. Abruptly, he snapped erect in his straps. He ripped out a savage oath.

"Kirk, that fiend never intended for me to be free! It was a torture and execution together. If I had grabbed that knife, not only you, but I also would have been electrocuted. It wouldn't be possible for such current to pass through me and kill you without killing me also!"

Kirkpatrick nodded, eyes still closed. "I suspected that," he said, "but I hoped he might have told me the truth. There was only one way to find out."

WITH A snarl of anger, Wentworth jammed the ropes against the knife again, sawed while the torturing electricity leaped and jerked through his body, sawed up and down until the ropes finally parted and his wrists came apart. He had to wait long, precious minutes while the swelling of his arms subsided. Then he folded his thumbs into his palms and strained on the straps. His wrists slipped; the leather gripped the flesh of his hands. The flesh tore, and his hands came free!

It was a work of moments then to throw the straps clear, to detach the electrode from the burned flesh of his calf and free Kirkpatrick. The Commissioner staggered to his feet. His hands bit into Wentworth's shoulder and keen, blue eyes stared deeply into eyes of gray-blue. Both men smiled a little, but neither said a word, Kirkpatrick's hands dropped and side by side, they stalked across the room to free Nita and Ram Singh. Toussaints Louvaine Wentworth did not untie.

"Kirk," he said, "would you take Nita and Ram Singh to the nearest road and commandeer two cars—one to take you to the telephone and the city so you can throw a guard around the dams, another for Ram Singh to bring back here?"

Kirkpatrick looked from Wentworth's grim face to the wry, mustached countenance of Toussaints Louvaine. He allowed a slight smile to lift his lip corners. He parted his own mustaches with thumb and forefinger and nodded. "Surely, Dick!"

Nita came to Wentworth's side for a moment. The tears were gone from her face now, and her eyes met his bravely. "You won't wait... too long, Dick," she whispered.

Wentworth shook his head, caught her in his arms for a hurried kiss and sent her away.

"Kirk," he called after his friend, "you'll remember it's balloons they usually employ, but don't depend on that exclusively. Anything that could touch the charged dams with wire would serve. One of those life-guard guns that shoots a line, for instance."

Then all were gone save Toussaints Louvaine and the Spider. Despite the calm movements, his deliberate voice, there was a mounting tension within him. Aronk Dong had said the dam would burst within an hour. Almost half that much time had elapsed while he fought his bonds. And Wentworth realized that what Kirkpatrick went to do was a futile gesture. The dams would burst; hundreds of homes would be swept away in the floods, their occupants drowned; the city would become a putrescent desert, unless—unless Aronk Dong died before the hour was out and the news was broadcast everywhere. With him dead, his men would be forced to abandon this terrific crime. They were men who had to have a dominating leader.

But what an impossible task for the Spider! To find Aronk Dong within a half-hour—to slay him and broadcast the news! Suddenly, Wentworth threw back his head and laughed. He wrenched Toussaints Louvaine from his bonds, herded him from the building. Ram Singh drove into the yard in a small sedan and Wentworth flung Louvaine into the back, climbed in beside him.

"Catch Kirkpatrick," he commanded the Hindu.

THE SEDAN whirled on two wheels in a skidding turn on the grass, jounced and clattered over the mud-holes of the road. Louvaine braced himself in a corner, but with ropes still securing his arms, he was helpless. He took out his rage in glaring.

As the car bounced onto smooth pavement and gathered speed, Wentworth turned to him.

"So far, Louvaine," he said amiably, "your offenses have been exclusively against me. You attempted to kill me and you kidnapped Miss Van Sloan. I think it might be arranged for you to be only deported, instead of answering for attempted murder and abduction."

The Frenchman's wry face twisted into a smile of self-mockery. "I was about to propose a trade," he answered agreeably, "my information for my life. I am, as you say, lick'. I take my medicine." The dapper Frenchman was rueful. " 'Ere is what I know. My men form contact wit' Aronk Dong through Brandon Early Electric *Campagnie.*"

"We haven't time to do that," Wentworth frowned.

"Anot'er t'ing," Louvaine continued. "I know this—alway'

when he sen' his lightnin', he himsel' make the signal. I t'ink that tonight he will be sure make the signal, and that is all I know."

Wentworth sat silently staring at the road ahead.

"I think that is *sahib* Kirkpatrick's car ahead," Ram Singh announced quietly. He began to flash his headlights off and on, off and on. He palmed the horn and the car ahead slowed. The door flung open and Kirkpatrick stepped out on the running board.

"I have a plan," Wentworth began rapidly as the cars drew abreast. "Aronk Dong said that he would have loudspeaker planes go all over the country announcing his plans. That means there must be a large number of planes equipped with the broadcasters ready. Commandeer those planes by phone and send them to every dam that backs up a New York reservoir. Have three cover New York City thoroughly. These planes are to spread the message that Aronk Dong is dead, killed by the Spider."

Kirkpatrick stared at him, frowning, then suddenly nodded. "It might work," he said and ducked back into the sedan.

"Don't forget to send them over the city, too!" Wentworth yelled after him and caught the wave of a hand in assent. "Ram Singh, get me to the nearest airport in nothing flat."

"It is an extra'nary good plan," Louvaine told Wentworth as the car sped toward a field. "You 'ope that the men at the dams will be frighten' and run away without wreckin' the dams. They will not t'ink it worth the risk to do such a t'ing when their leader is dead. But 'ave you thought of this? That there may be some who will wait for the signal? If they see that signal they will know that you lie. They will know that Aronk Dong is alive and they will be afraid not to destroy the dams."

Wentworth nodded slowly. Louvaine had grasped his plan, even as Kirkpatrick had, once he had outlined the action. It was a good plan, but there was a chance that most of the men would fear to flee their posts before the time for the signal had come and gone. That was why he would have the planes prowl back and forth across the city itself, shouting down into the street with broadcasting equipment which magnified the voice a million times: "Aronk Dong is dead! The Spider killed him!"

If Aronk Dong had not already arranged for a spectacular signal, the boastful lie would prick his vanity and drive him to action. Wentworth hoped, and admitted the hope was frail, that he might spot the signal at its birth and destroy both it and the Lion Man.

At the air field, Wentworth suddenly decided to take Toussaints Louvaine with him. It was possible the man had not told everything. He might force some further word from him. Ram Singh bowed before Wentworth, lifted beseeching eyes.

"*Sahib*, master!" his Hindustani sputtered rapidly. "You go to face the enemy without thy bodyguard?"

WENTWORTH DID not stop strapping on the parachute-pack. He was conscious of each racing moment.

"I have another task for you, O my warrior! It may be thou shalt be the one to trap the monster. Go thou and telephone Professor Brownlee. Ask of him what he discovered from his tests. Then hasten thou to the city and watch for me." He broke into harsh Hindustani, speaking swiftly, then swung up into the cockpit, in the front well of which he had already placed Louvaine. Seconds later, the ship shot down the tarmac and swept into a steep climb back toward the city.

Wentworth opened the throttle until the plane's motor quivered with speed—until the tachometer needled near the danger point. The landscape below was a black, continuous blur. Lights were streaks. Wentworth had not wasted time in climbing. He needed only a thousand feet of altitude and he would get that by slow degrees as he howled across the night sky.

He had had ear-phones placed on the Frenchman's head and now, gripping the stick between his knees, he adjusted those in his own cockpit. During the endless ten minutes of his race for New York, he questioned Louvaine ceaselessly, but got no more information.

Wentworth had his own idea as to the type of signal Aronk Dong would use. What could be more spectacular than a vivid flash of lightning across the clear unclouded, night sky? It was obvious, since he intended the destruction of the dams tonight, that he was not dependent upon approaching thunder storms to generate his electricity. Moreover, if not a lightning flash, then what signal could he use that would be visible at all the dams that stored up water for the city? The more Wentworth thought of it, the more he became convinced that lightning would be the signal; lightning over New York!

A feeling of helplessness gripped him. He had just one chance. If there were open metal-work on the thing at which Aronk Dong would hurl his lightnings, that structure would glitter with small, blue, electric flames a few moments before the lightning blast. If he could spot that, then intercept the balloon....

Wentworth was over the city now, swinging low across the roof-tops. The hilly Bronx with its squat brick apartments slid past beneath him—the ribbon of the Harlem Ship Canal, then the dark oblong of Central Park with its limpid lakes.

Wentworth caught the green-and-red running-lights of three other planes patrolling north and south over the city. He darted near enough to one of them to hear the stentorian bellow of its broadcaster even above the roar of his engine:

"Aronk Dong is dead! The Spider killed him!"

A taut smile twisted Wentworth's lips. If those words did not prove prophetic, the whole city would curse his name tomorrow with thirst-bloated tongues and lips. Pestilence and fire would rage through the streets. Even if the Spider struck then, it would be too late for countless hundreds in the valleys below the dams. No, no! He must find his enemy now, within the next five minutes and destroy him; he must prevent the signal. There could be no talk of failure.

BACK AND forth, not a hundred feet above the roof-tops, Wentworth swept. Damn it, he should have had Kirkpatrick turn out all the lights. Then that faint, blue flicker would be brilliant against the city's dead-velvet black. But now colors and lights danced and flashed. Its brilliance reached far up into the heavens so that light lay in a smoky glow over the city canyons and the rearing roof tops. It clouded his vision.

Northward now, along the West Side, above the berths of long ships, above the express highway that climbed and poured its gush of light-flashing autos into Riverside Drive. Up the twisting course of the Drive beside towering apartment houses. There was the Riverside Tower, where Nita's high apartment stared with blank windows out over the river. By the heavens! Was that flicker of blue?

Wentworth swung in a sweeping bank, eyes straining. But it was there no more. He had fooled himself. He swung on up the Hudson, cut sharply back across Manhattan and down the East River, past the rocky cliffs of Hellgate, over low-lying Welfare Island where was the city prison.

Wentworth rubbed his fingers against thumb, brushed his palm against his thigh. There was a sharp, cruel throbbing in his throat—the beating of his heart! Minutes were kicking past. The hour was finished, but still there came no smashing gleam of lightning on the northern horizon. The dams still stood; the signal had not been given. Perhaps, it would not be given—perhaps Aronk Dong was terrified to learn that the men he had left to die had escaped the trap... But that was a vain hope.

Then where was the signal? Wentworth leaned over the left side of his cockpit, staring down at the black East River with its shimmering rows of reflected lights. Would the flash come from Brooklyn, over on the tip of Long Island? Suddenly, instinctively, Wentworth threw his plane into a sharp, left bank. He was positive this time that out of the corner of his eye, he had caught a flicker of blue. By God! He was right! There it was again, a shimmer of blue. It was Aronk Dong's blue, electric fire! And it danced its hellish jig of doom over the wires and braces of the Queensborough Bridge, longest and biggest of the bridges that span the East River between Manhattan and Long Island! That was where Aronk Dong had chosen to herald his mad conquest of the world!

CHAPTER 18
DEATH'S AUCTION

WENTWORTH'S FACE was set in a mould of granite. He had only seconds now—heartbeats of time—to locate the spot from which the fiend's lightning would strike at the bridge!

Back there in the hills, Wentworth knew, similar blue fire performed its death-dance over the dams that held back billions of gallons of water. Unless he could prevent this flash, those raging floods would sweep over the land. And tomorrow, New York City would be without any water at all…!

He was over the Queensborough Bridge, sweeping up its length. The wind was from the East—from over Long Island, but Wentworth saw at once that the hell sparks were closest and hottest over the span between Welfare Island and Manhattan. How could a balloon be aimed to drift along the eastern end of the bridge and finally make the contact on the western half? From what point would such a balloon be released?

Wentworth cursed as, with engine revving at top speed, he slashed back and forth over the Long Island shore—swept low over Welfare Island. Surely it would be impossible for Aronk Dong to operate from the armed prison-fortress into which the island had been turned! He could not carry his equipment there, inflate and release his balloon. No, no! It was not on Welfare Island that he must seek his prey. It was on Manhattan, New York City itself! What, against the wind? Was the balloon to drift against the wind?

Oaths poured from Wentworth's lips in a ragged stream. Just why did he think that a balloon was to be used? He himself had told Kirkpatrick that anything that could carry a wire to the point of contact would suffice. With the thought, he raced toward the Manhattan shore, conscious of the high-leaping sparks along the bridge, knowing that it would be only seconds now before Aronk Dong flashed the signal that would mean more death and disease and famine than even a war could bring to this great city.

He swept upward in a steep climb, and then, high against the night sky—*he saw the balloon!* It floated almost stationary. It was downwind from the bridge. Immediately, Wentworth strove for more ceiling. He saw that the balloon was still rising. Trailing from it, a thin wire led off toward one of the apartments spiring above Sutton Place.

Grimly, Wentworth determined that if bullets failed, he would fly his plane through the balloon and take a chance on being able to land the damaged ship. Louvaine would have to take his chances for life along with the Spider.

He climbed, and it seemed to him that the balloon was racing with him, trying to soar faster than the plane. Wentworth laughed. Suddenly he understood the Lion Man's plan. The flash must come from the heavens, yet he feared more target practice such as Wentworth had worked on his five balloons this same day. So the balloon floated downwind and a coast guard gun would fire the other end of the balloon's wire across the charged bridge.

Aronk Dong would not miss. The wire would carry the flash upward into the night sky. The severed braces of the bridge would spill traffic and men into the river. Far off to North, men would read the message of that forked streak across the sky. They would know that the shouting planes had lied and that Aronk Dong was alive. They would loose the lightning on the dams—desolation….

But Wentworth's sky-boring plane had reached the balloon now. Circling it, scarcely more than a wing's length away, Wentworth emptied his automatic through the fabric. The balloon danced and dipped in the beat of lead, but it did not fall. Swiftly, gripping the stick between his knees as he circled, Wentworth stuffed a new clip into the automatic, yanked back the bolt and snicked a cartridge into the chamber. Once more he swept close, poured lead through the balloon.

IT BOWED to him as gracefully as a lady, bobbing its bulbous head. Was he mistaken, or was the balloon a little—*smaller?* Once more Wentworth reloaded and fired. This time there could be no doubt about it. The balloon had lost fifty feet of elevation. Suddenly, as he watched, the fabric sparked into flame, yellow flame that licked up and consumed the bag in a breath. Static electricity had ignited the hydrogen gas—electricity generated by the rush of the gas escaping through the rents Wentworth's bullets had made.

That first bud of spark was all that Wentworth waited to

The point of the sword slid beneath Louvaine's chin—half the blade followed it!

see. He threw his ship into a sharp dive, spurting toward the apartment house from which the wire had trailed. Destruction of the balloon would not thwart Aronk Dong. He could send up another, or perhaps he could fire his gun even with the wire trailing over the water. Either way would discharge the pent-up electricity in the bridge—would flash the fatal signal northward.

Wentworth picked up the mouthpiece of the headset that connected him with Louvaine. "I'm going to land on that penthouse terrace," he stated, words clipped.

"You're mad! *Fou!*" Louvaine screamed. A torrent of frenzied French poured out.

Wentworth jerked off his headset and jockeyed the plane. His quick eyes had caught the one possibility of reaching Aronk Dong before the Lion Man could hurl lightning across the skies. He must land on the terrace from which the Lord of the Lightnings planned to destroy bridge and dams and city all in one swift breath! If Louvaine could have seen Wentworth's eyes then, he would have been certain, even as he had screamed, the Spider was mad!

Wentworth hurled the ship straight toward disaster. There was no hope of landing on that terrace, although it was fifty feet square. Yet Wentworth knew he must do it and live afterward to kill Aronk Dong. His automatic, loaded once more, he thrust into the breast of his leather flying-tunic.

He knew just what he planned to do, how he would land on that tiny space. It was too narrow even to side-slip, kill his speed, and straighten out to a normal landing. No, that would ram his nose against the side of the building, shove the hot motor back in his lap! What he planned was even more dangerous—a wild and desperate chance which *must* succeed....

He dipped far below the level of the terrace, pulled back the stick and sent the ship climbing at an impossible angle, headed for a stall. Within seconds, it would lose flying speed, slide off on one wing into a tail spin and dash itself to pieces on the rocky shore below.

Dead ahead of him was the apartment wall. There was no chance at all of diving out of his stall that way. But Wentworth had no intention of doing that. His iron nerves, his tensed muscles held the plane true. He saw lights blazing from windows—apparently under him now—but his eyes were fixed on the edge of the terrace now only fifty feet above him, now thirty... twenty... *Now!*

The plane swooped up over the edge of the terrace wall. Wentworth's steady hand pointed the nose straight upward, stalled it dead in the air, ten feet above the terrace floor. The ship swung off to the side. Wentworth held that wing down, let it crumple to break the fall. The ship smacked against the wall of the penthouse, bounced halfway across the terrace and settled on smashed landing gear. *He had landed on the terrace!*

Wentworth jerked painfully against the safety straps. His head slammed against the crash pad. But the instant the ship had settled, he threw off the leather bands and vaulted to the terrace. He did not wait to look at Louvaine. The Frenchman would have to care for himself. For Wentworth had seen a man dart toward the double French doors of the terrace even as the plane had stood on its tail, and that man had a flowing mane!

Wentworth stumbled. His head reeled with dizziness, but he drove himself across the tiled terrace, reached the double doors and swayed there. The man was Aronk Dong, all right. He was plunging across the room toward a white rope that lay across the floor. Wentworth knew instantly what it was—the firing lanyard of a coast guard gun! He snatched out the heavy automatic from his tunic and smashed bitter lead across the room.

HE WAS still dazed from the shock of that crackup and his lead went wild, but Aronk Dong dodged at the shot. He swerved away from the lanyard, sprang toward a desk where a revolver lay. Wentworth steadied himself, gripped the automatic. Tonight, when he should be strongest and surest, his hand felt numb. Dizziness whirled the room about him. He fought for steadiness, crouched above his automatic….

But Aronk Dong did not pause when he seized the revolver. He pounded straight on through a door beyond the table. With a curse, Wentworth lunged forward to hurl himself into the pursuit. On the point of springing through the doorway, he checked himself. It was instinct—the instinct of a thousand grim battles—that stopped him in mid-rush. Hot lead burned through from the other room—within inches of his face.

Wentworth seized his automatic with his left hand, thrust it around the edge of the doorjamb and swept bullets across the other room. The penthouse was suddenly full of the crash of guns. Walls shivered with reverberations. Lead smashed a lamp behind Wentworth with a crash and tinkle of broken glass. Another bullet lashed splinters from the door-facing and Wentworth felt the burn of the flying wood on his temple.

He fired again, blindly. His hand was flung back from the door-jamb. There was a numb feeling as if his hand was no longer attached to his wrist. His gun skated across the floor. He stared down at his left hand. The Lion Man's bullet had hit his gun.

Sudden rage heated Wentworth's brain. Its fire drove the daze from his senses. His shoulders hunched, he barged toward the doorway.

Aronk Dong was heaving through it, swinging his pistol's muzzle toward Wentworth as he dashed by. Wentworth swung his fist, caught the Lion Man behind the ear and sent him reeling. The revolver spun from his hand. Instantly, Wentworth sprang after him. He forced coordination into his shocked body by sheer, concentrated will power.

The Spider knew that if the Lion Man could get free of him, he would yank that lanyard, flash that fateful signal to his men. The thought lent Wentworth strength, fed fuel to his rage. He brushed Aronk Dong, slugging a looping right. The Lion Man half-blocked the blow, raked at Wentworth's head with a clawed hand. One sweep—ripping open his face and throat—and he would be dead!

Groping behind him, Wentworth grasped the overturned lamp with his right hand. He snatched it up, hurled it in a single movement. The base was heavy, the throw was hurried, but nevertheless, the lamp caught Aronk Dong on the chest and checked him, made him stagger backward.

Wentworth's eyes flashed about, seeking a weapon. He saw that the walls were hung with heavy, ancient swords; a thrill of pleasure shot through him. There was a round, sturdy shield that would block those ripping claws, and there was a short Roman sword of shiny steel. He reached the wall in a long leap, ripped the shield down, slid his left arm through the straps.

Aronk Dong saw him snatch shield and sword, started forward in a rush, then checked himself. With an answering snarl of rage, he sprang to the opposite wall of the room, snatched down a huge, two-handed crusaders' sword, a *flambage,* flame-blade, with waved edges. He flung it high over his head, rushing in to strike. For a moment, as light caught the steel, it seemed that Aronk Dong clutched in his hands one of his own lightning bolts!

ARONK DONG struck like a flash of lightning, the *flambage* sweeping down with terrific force, striking at Wentworth's head. Wentworth's shield surged high, covering head and shoulder. The sword clashed like a sledge on an anvil, skidded off Wentworth's skillfully slanted protector. Wentworth stepped under the stroke. His short sword snicked upward toward the Lion Man's body. Not more than two feet long, it could move swiftly. The thrust was snake-quick.

But the Lion Man had not waited to learn the results of his blow. He had leaped backward and even as the sword clanged on shield. He was two yards away from the thrust and once more the sword was sweeping upward and over.

"Ver' pretty, *m'sieurs,*" a voice jeered from the doorway behind Wentworth. "Ver' pretty indeed. *Très, très joli!* I like ver' much the play with swords."

Wentworth cursed under his breath, bracing his thighs to take the slam of the heavy blade, rushing in with a hacking thrust of the short sword. Once more Aronk Dong leaped clear, bouncing his shoulders against the wall and springing past Wentworth. As he passed, he tried a hacking side-swing of the long blade, but the shield met that, too. Wentworth followed closely, trying to strike before the Lion Man could recover.

As he whirled, he caught a glimpse of Toussaints Louvaine across the room. The Frenchman held the white gun lanyard in his hands. He was smiling, his small mustaches an exclamation point of mirth. There was a smear of blood across his cheek, but it only gave him a devil-may-care quirkiness.

"Don't, fool!" Wentworth shouted. "That lanyard will fire a gun and destroy the bridge, signal the men at the dams! Drop it!"

"You do not wish me to pull the lanyard, eh, Spider?" Toussaints Louvaine was gibing. "How much is it wort' to you not to pull it, Spider?"

"A million if you *do* pull it, Louvaine!" Aronk Dong cried, triumph deepening his voice.

"Two millions if you *don't* pull it, Louvaine!" Wentworth panted.

Louvaine would do just as he said, Wentworth knew—sell out to the highest bidder. And he would not hesitate to fire the gun. A man who would sell a fearful weapon of war against his own mother country—because his own land could not bid high enough for the weapon—would not scruple to loose the floods of death and desolation upon the city.

"Two million I'm bid! Two million I'm bid!" Louvaine chanted. "Throw in another million and I might even trip up this Lion Man when he isn't looking. Or make it four million, Aronk Dong, and I'll do a like service for you."

Wentworth's back was to Louvaine. He slid a blow from his shield cleverly, and while his enemy was off balance, leaped forward. His shield was against the other's sword arm, holding off a possible blow. His own blade was streaking in. A punch on the side of the head hurled Wentworth aside. He swayed dizzily on his feet, barely caught himself in time to turn a thrust from a slapping blade, then once more he was on guard.

"That is not fair, *M'sieur* Spider," Louvaine mocked, walking back to the lanyard. "You would have settle' the fight before the auction was over and that I cannot permit. Take care les' I interfere again."

ONCE MORE Wentworth and Aronk Dong were fighting on equal terms. Sweat streaked their faces. Wentworth's arms felt like lead wearied by the unaccustomed weight of the weapons he wielded. The floor underfoot was slippery, waxed hardwood, and rugs had been kicked into dangerous obstacles.

"Well, *gentilhommes?*" Louvaine queried, "the las' bid was that of *M'sieur* Wentworth at two millions, but I 'ave now an additional value to offer—my interference! I could take another of these swords…."

"Four million, damn you!" Aronk Dong panted. "Pull the lanyard; then help me kill this fool."

"But your security, *mon ami,*" Louvaine murmured gently. "What guarantee do I 'ave that you will pay?"

"The security of a man with a firearm over one without any,"

Aronk Dong snapped. "That is your guarantee. The money is here in the apartment. Pull, man! Pull the lanyard!"

Wentworth, swinging to dodge a new attack, saw Louvaine's face, saw in his expression that he had accepted the Lion Man's offer. Wentworth saw, too, that Louvaine gripped the Lion Man's revolver in his right hand.

"Which shall it be, firs', Aronk Dong?" Louvaine whispered softly. "The Spider, or the lanyard?"

"The lanyard, man, the lanyard!"

As he spoke, Wentworth sprang straight backward a full two yards. His move had caught Aronk Dong unprepared and for the moment, the Spider was in the clear. He jerked his short sword up over his shoulder and hurled it violently, the weight of his shoulders and body behind it Aronk Dong saw what was happening and shrieked a warning. Toussaints Louvaine did not see until too late.

The point of the sword slid in beneath his chin; half the two-foot blade followed it. The weight of the blow slammed the dapper Frenchman backward, jerked his feet up into the air. Before they clapped back to the floor, Toussaints Louvaine was dead, the sword rammed through his throat.

Aronk Dong cried out in bellowing triumph as he saw Wentworth empty-handed. He leaped forward, swinging the long sword high above his head with both hands. Wentworth snatched the shield from his arm and hurled it violently. It caught the Lion Man's left arm as it came down, knocked that hand clear of the sword.

But the blade was flashing down now! One hand could guide

it, did guide it truly for Wentworth's head! He flung himself into a backward leap, dived through a doorway into the next room. The sword gouged into the wooden facing, snapped off clean. Before Wentworth could spring back to the attack, Aronk Dong snatched the door and slammed it shut in his face.

Wentworth heard the lock thrown and hurled himself violently against the barrier. It quivered, but held. The Spider went mad then.

Within brief moments, Aronk Dong would seize that lanyard and blast the city with one tug. The door would not yield beneath his assault. He needed something heavy… His eye caught a solidly built oak table. He was across the room in a bound, snatching it up. He set it on his shoulder and charged the door.

It shook, cracked, but still did not fall. Once more Wentworth charged with his battering ram. As he slammed again into the door, he heard a pistol shot from the next room. It was drowned instantly in the crashing explosion as the door shattered and swung lop-sided on its hinges. Wentworth charged through into the next room, stopped dead and let the table clatter down.

Aronk Dong lay upon the floor, his glazed eyes staring straight upward. The revolver was still clutched in Toussaints Louvaine's dead hand. And Aronk Dong had been shot through the chest!

CHAPTER 19
BENEATH THE LION'S MANE

FOR FULLY half a minute, Wentworth stared down at the two men on the floor; then he hurled across the room to the terrace, streaked for the railing. He stared out into the night. Queensborough Bridge still stood. The gun—where was the gun? He flung a searching look about, ran back into the house to trace the lanyard. Until the charge was drawn from that gun....

Inside the door, Wentworth stepped rigidly, staring at the two men—Louvaine with the sword thrust entirely through his neck. A curse ripped from Wentworth's lips. How could a man with a sword through his neck shoot down another? He knew, even as he put the question to himself, that it was impossible. Louvaine had not shot Aronk Dong. Then who...?

Wentworth flung to the Lion Man and crouched over him. Life was still in the body. His breath came in rough, rapid exhalations. Suddenly, violently, a door across the room flung open and Bets Decker darted in. She clutched an automatic in her right hand and she ran straight across toward Wentworth. Behind her pelted blonde Alice Auruckner on high-heeled shoes. As on the first occasion when he had seen her, she was all in gray, like a small, pert squirrel. But there was no blonde cuteness in her face. It was drawn and white, her eyes haggard.

Just before she reached Wentworth, Bets Decker swerved aside. She crossed to the lanyard in a leap and snatched it up.

"If you take a step toward me, I'll pull it," she cried. "Hurry,

Alice, get Bud on his feet and out of here. You there, Wentworth, help carry him out."

Wentworth smiled thinly. He got to his feet with a lurch, and took a long stride toward Bets Decker. She dropped her automatic and seized the lanyard with both hands, held it dangerously taut. Her black eyes seemed twice their natural size. They dominated her pale, curl-ringed face like brilliant lamps.

"You know what will happen if I pull this," she yelled. "For God's sake don't force me to do it!" There was a desperation in her voice that convinced Wentworth.

"Don't be silly," he said mildly, smiling. "You know that you don't want to kill all the people that will die if you pull that rope."

"No, I don't!" she agreed tensely. Her fine, red lips moved very little, showing her white, locked teeth. "I don't, but I will if you don't help me get Bud out of here. He couldn't help the things he did. He went out of his head because people wouldn't recognize his genius. He swore he'd make them believe in him. He really couldn't help it. And you've got to help us get him out of here."

"Certainly," Wentworth agreed ironically. "Anything to get you away from that lanyard." He pretended unconcern, but his heart was a fluttering, frightened thing—not for himself, but for the untold millions. Damn it, the girl was as tense as a piano wire. If anyone spoke suddenly, she might yank that lanyard—all hell would blaze within seconds.

"I'll help you," he said, "but let go of that lanyard. Listen, I swear to you that I'll help you."

"Never mind," a man's quiet voice said from the doorway.

Wentworth saw Bets Decker's head jerk that way, saw her

arms tighten. He hurled himself forward frantically. His hand caught the girl's shoulder and spun her aside, his other hand held the lanyard so that she could not yank it. He leaned back against the wall and wiped a hand across his beaded forehead.

"Kirk," he said hoarsely to the man in the door, "will you, for God's sake, please send somebody to the other end of this lanyard to draw the charge? If it's fired, Queensborough Bridge will be wrecked by lightning. That will signal the men at the dams...."

Kirkpatrick issued a curt order and two of his men advanced. One stood over the lanyard with braced feet and a drawn gun and the other carefully traced the line. He disappeared into the darkness of the terrace. Bets Decker was sobbing. But she did not approach the Lion Man lying on the floor. She held her shoulders against the wall, sobbed dry sobs. No tears traced her face. On her knees on the floor, Alice Auruckner was stroking Bud Early's forehead.

"So it was Bud Early after all," Kirkpatrick rasped from the doorway. "The plane crash was reported; I guessed it was you." ALICE HAD stripped the wig and mustaches from Early's pale face and was whispering low to him. She had made a pad of an insignificant handkerchief, put it over the wound in his chest. Wentworth saw that Horace Jones and another man he recognized instantly as Cosmo Delane, the laboratory expert he had suspected, were with Kirkpatrick. Ram Singh was behind him.

The loyal Hindu came across the room swiftly and whispered in his ear. Wentworth's lips twitched and began to smile. Horace Jones crossed to Alice and put his big hands under her arms.

"Get up, darling," he muttered softly. "Bud is dead."

Wentworth dropped to his knees beside Early, picked up his right hand and felt the pulse. It was fluttering, but it was fairly positive. The wound was high up—not especially dangerous. A steel claw hung from a cord at the wrist. It was ordinarily up the sleeve, but when the wearer struck, the paw dropped into his palm. Fastened to the right index finger was a small mechanical ratchet such as is used on cigarette lighters. When the second and third fingers of the hand pulled at a wire, the ratchet spun and made sparks. That, then, was how the Lion Man had made his finger spark. The shocks must have been administered by hidden plates in the floor, possibly operated by the Chinese.

Wentworth looked up sharply at Kirkpatrick. "Did you find the Chinese?"

Kirkpatrick nodded grimly. "Ram Singh did," he said. "With his knife! The beggar was ready to ambush us."

Wentworth nodded absently, bent across Early's body and stripped the sleeve from the man's left arm. He looked at the flesh of the forearm, clear and unbruised, then he stood erect and smiled thinly into Horace Jones' face.

"You, Jones," he accused clearly, "are Aronk Dong, the Lion Man, the Lord of the Lightnings, you damned murderer!"

A startled hush filled the room. Jones looked at Wentworth in amazement. "Are you crazy?" he demanded. "There lies Bud Early on the floor, with all the trappings of the Man from Mars, and you call me the Lion Man! You must be crazy!"

Wentworth grated flatly. "No, it isn't a joke. What brought you here?"

"I followed Alice Auruckner," Jones snarled, suddenly furious, "if it's any of your damn' business. I was calling on her this evening. I saw her leave the house with Bets Decker and followed her here."

Wentworth's face was utterly passive. The policeman who straddled the lanyard and Kirkpatrick were watching the scene with alert eyes.

"Ram Singh has been following you ever since you left the club," Wentworth revealed slowly. "How long, O Ram Singh, has this carrion been in the building?"

"Ever since he left the club, *sahib*," Ram Singh answered in his harsh, nasal voice.

"This is conspiracy!" Jones cried. He turned, flung a swift glance about the room. Only Alice Auruckner was not looking at him. She rocked Bud Early's head in her lap. Bets Decker was staring at Jones with wide eyes.

"No, Jones. Not a conspiracy," Wentworth drawled. "Just an exposing of the truth. Where have you been, Jones, while all these horrors were going on?"

"The newspapers should tell you," Jones replied shortly. "They're running a series of my articles on Aronk Dong. You know that. I've been up at my Connecticut place writing that stuff."

"All this time, Jones?"

"All this time." Jones was angrily insistent. "My agent can tell you that the stuff has been coming in day by day."

"It is a curious thing about your manuscripts, Jones," Wentworth went on softly. "I wondered at their uncanny accuracy. I went so far as to get hold of some of the copy and compare it with specimens from your typewriter up in Connecticut. It was written on that machine all right, but here's a curious thing..." He paused, eyeing Jones. "I had your typewriter removed from your premises and tested. The condition of the oil and the ribbon reveal that *it hasn't been used for a month.*

"You see what that means, don't you, Jones? It means that you wrote about Aronk Dong *before such a creature had ever been heard of.*

"No, it won't do, Jones. Only a writer such as yourself could have created so fantastic a character and expected to make him convincing. No one else would have realized that there are hundreds of thousands of persons in the country who would accept the reality of that character.

"You stole Bud Early's invention and murdered with it while you held him a prisoner. You had him hidden here, planned to murder him in your disguise and let him shoulder the blame. You almost succeeded. You went farther than that—you stole and seduced his secretary, little Bets Decker, making her think that you were Bud Early in disguise. She had been in love with Bud for a long time."

HORACE JONES contrived a laugh, flung an appreciative glance at Bets Decker. "Thanks for the compliment, at any rate," he said. "If you are quite through with all this, I think I'll be going."

"Bets," cried Wentworth, "how did he explain the fact that he tortured you?"

Bets Decker pulled her haggard eyes from Horace Jones' face

to Wentworth. "It was a test," she said, whispering. "A test of my loyalty!"

"So," Wentworth said, "he almost twisted off your arms."

He turned from her to Kirkpatrick. "I fought with Aronk Dong up here, with that shield and that short sword that killed Louvaine over there. I flung my shield at Aronk Dong and struck him on the left forearm so hard that it tore his hold loose from his sword. Such a blow would leave a mark of some kind. You can see for yourself that Bud Early's arm is not bruised." He whirled to Jones.

"Jones, roll up your sleeve!"

With a hoarse cry, Jones sprang for the open terrace doors.

"Stop!" Kirkpatrick shouted. He snatched for his gun, but his coat got in the way. It was Bets Decker who snatched an automatic from the floor. Still on her knees, holding her gun in both hands, she squeezed the trigger until the gun clicked emptily in her hand. Horace Jones took the whole magazine between his shoulders. He stumbled, choked a scream, and fell forward on his face.

Wentworth leaped toward the girl, but she was on her feet, running like a deer. He saw her pale face twist about once, toward the picture of Alice Auruckner and Bud Early upon the floor, then she was gone. She reached the parapet ten feet ahead of him, sprang to its top. Even as he snatched for her ankles, she swan-dived off into space.

It was the first time Wentworth had ever witnessed anyone fall so far silently. But that was how Bets Decker went down, silent—a graceful swan-dive to death. It was worse that way somehow. The poor kid had loved Bud Early, slaved for him, given him up to the blonde....

Wentworth went heavily back toward the penthouse, toward the men bunched in the doorway over the bullet-riddled body. He looked down at Horace Jones, the man who had planned to conquer the world by fear—and smiled. Fear, such as Aronk Dong had brewed, was strong medicine. But there were others, stronger still. Among them were love and faith—and courage!